MY HOUSE IS FALLING DOWN

Mary Loudon

PICADOR

First published 2019 by Picador
an imprint of Pan Macmillan
20 New Wharf Road, London N1 9RR
Associated companies throughout the world
www.panmacmillan.com

ISBN 978-1-5290-0527-1

The lyrics from 'Feeling Good' and 'Goldfinger' quoted on page 129
were written by Leslie Bricusse and Anthony Newley. The lyrics for
'When I'm Sixty Four' on page 213 were written by Paul McCartney.
The quotation from *The Life of Brian* on page 224 was written by the
members of Monty Python.

9 8 7 6 5 4 3 2 1

A CIP catalogue record for this book is available from the British Library.

Typeset in Athelas by Palimpsest Book Production Ltd, Falkirk, Stirlingshire
Printed and bound by CPI Group (UK) Ltd, Croydon, CR0 4YY

Visit **www.picador.com** to read more about all our books
and to buy them. You will also find features, author interviews and
news of any author events, and you can sign up for e-newsletters
so that you're always first to hear about our new releases.

For James

Wherever there is a human being,
there is an opportunity for crisis.

SENECA

When in doubt, tell the truth.

MARK TWAIN

Looking back, I find it difficult to understand exactly when the relationship began but if there was a defining moment I think it was when I first made a concession for him.

On the morning that I drove under a sullen sky to the local railway station instead of walking the children to school, a decision was made. It was the first day of term after the Christmas holidays. Rightly, my hands should have been full. Yet I left my husband to ensure that by 8.20 everybody was fed, moderately happy and out of the house – in a daily ritual that holds something approaching religious significance for me – and forsook breakfast with my family for a train that delivered me to London decently in time to eat croissants, with Angus. It was, I noticed when checking my diary, the Feast of the Epiphany. A day given over to revelation: you couldn't make it up.

But it could easily have been earlier. It might have been the evening I responded to an email from Angus with more than best wishes, taking my lead, I guess, from his beginning *Dear You* and ending *A xxx*. And it would be difficult convincingly to discount the numerical significance (let alone any other kind) of two

I

hundred further emails and texts – give or take – that shot back and forth between us during the ensuing month; and those, too, after only one public encounter, during which a large pot of tea topped the drinks bill and I kept my overcoat on.

After that, at our first private meeting (assignation? tryst? – I still don't really know what to call it), this time at Angus's home, we might have shared our first kiss had I not inclined my face to one side as he moved slowly towards me. He kissed my hair instead and then, with a lightness of touch I no longer associate with him but the directness that I do, he brushed the back of his right hand across my right cheek. And as he raised that hand in a diagonal across my body, in the briefest of moments I knew what was coming and yearned, as if I had an hour in which to anticipate it, for the warm skim of his curled fingers on my skin.

Silently, I implored, *Don't take your hand away*. He took his hand away. He suggested we go to the kitchen to look at the view of the light falling across the busy river. He made tea, toasted some muffins, and we talked until it was dark; about music, food, and then love. Later, he put his arms around my waist and pulled me to him, trembling.

I nearly said, 'I know your game.'

He said, 'You are exquisite.'

The very first time I saw him: at a party, for the

opening of a new art gallery. I arrived in a light mood, unguarded. Within fifteen minutes Angus had happened. Introduced, he stopped talking to the person he was with and for longer than is customary on such occasions he gazed at me. My husband was with me – it was a work party for him, at which I was his guest – and I think they shook hands. I'm pretty sure they must have done for they both have impeccable manners. I do remember that with casual efficiency they established which other guests present were the ones with whom they shared an acquaintance. Like card dealers at a gaming table, shuffling packs in butterfly arcs as an artful prelude to their distribution, Angus and my husband deftly rearranged the assembled company into meaningful subsets because it was the only competitive game available to them at that moment, and they're both competitive men. That's how people like Angus and my husband pass the time at parties they affect to dislike but attend nonetheless.

Meanwhile, I gazed back at this beautiful man, wordless – though stupefied would be the word. Stupefied is what I told Angus, weeks later. He raised questions about my choice of adjective. He thought stupefied a little blunt, lacking in scope. He likes words with dimensions. So do I, as it happens. Yet even when I presented to him a generous range of alternatives that the word embraces – bewildered, dazed, bemused, amazed, confused, astonished, stunned, impressed – he did not recant. Not until, sufficiently irritated with him, I insisted he look it up. After that, he withdrew his objections, grinning, pleased with himself to have had that effect.

Looking back, I realize that it simply doesn't matter – the when and where it all began: at a party; over tea in a cafe; in Angus's unfamiliar, watery home; or perhaps most significantly during a thousand small-hour disclosures, half of them my own, feverishly typed on a laptop in the dim light of a muted kitchen. It's irrelevant. I fell in love so inordinately that time and place mean nothing. Like carbon dating, deciphering love's earliest imprint is an imprecise business. When and where provide history and geography but only why conveys anything worthwhile. Only why is significant and only why matters. Like why, when I knew so little of him still, I would allow a man who is not my husband to declare himself to me, except that he recognized me for what I am: a woman at odds with herself.

Nevertheless, until I left my family eating breakfast that morning and walked out of our house in Angus's favour, I could reasonably well convince myself that nothing had altered significantly. Turning the key in the front door later that night, I might as well have been turning my own self-delusion on its head. It was fifteen hours that I'd been gone and they were all asleep when I returned.

I have thought about it often, how easy it was to walk out of the door, empty-handed. Much later, redefined by the trauma of enchantment, I had a more punishing move to make.

The time of the concert is not lost on me: a lunchtime recital at the Queen Elizabeth Hall. 1 p.m., safe as houses. Angus's email asking whether I'd like to go with him arrived a week before the concert's date, and in my book a week is no time at all to make a plan of that kind. In my book – an A4 lined diary bought from my village shop – there are biro-scrawled work appointments I must honour that stretch several months ahead, though admittedly some of them are moveable feasts and I don't work every day. As it happens, I have work arranged for the day Angus suggests but in this instance, I change it. It's a risk and a foolish one: my client is new and the commission quite big. I feel badly about messing her around but evidently not badly enough to behave better.

Angus texts: '*Is it okay with your husband?*'

'It doesn't bother me who you listen to music with,' Mark says, when I ask him. 'It's never going to be me, is it?'

'But does Angus bother you?'

5

Mark shrugs.

'Why would he?'

I text: *'I wouldn't come if it weren't okay.'*

I think about the last time I went to a concert in London, when my brother was conducting. I went alone, described it afterwards to Mark; I told him again how music has always provided such succour for me. I said I remembered learning in physics that every object has a natural frequency at which it will vibrate when struck. I tried to explain that a lot of music produced in me the same powerful reaction, and whether proposed by a community of instruments or a solo voice, its impact was so perfectly matched to my sense of the sublime that momentarily I would experience the seemingly impossible – a feeling of being perfectly met and in tune, wanting for nothing on earth but the moment itself.

I said, 'Does that make any kind of sense to you?'

He said, 'I'm not sure. It sounds a bit like fantastic sex.'

'I so wish I could share it with you.'

'Me too, babe, but it's never going to happen.'

On the day of the concert there is a mighty freeze. It is not the first of the season but it's the most severe so far; the trees are blanched, their twigs crystalline. From the freezer, I remove a fish pie that I made last week and put it to one side to defrost. I clear what's left of breakfast and empty the washing machine of Mark's jeans and the twins' PE kits. I drape their small, navy shorts on a drying rack. *My babies.* I shake Mark's jeans, smooth the pocket linings and pull out the creases. *My man.* Hanging laundry makes me sentimental. Upstairs, I make beds, picking up stray soft animals and littered felt-tip pens. My movements are automatic. I love these daily devotions, this liturgy of the hours. I shower quickly, and still wrapped in my towel I print out the month's invoices and put them into already stamped, addressed envelopes. I'll post them when I go to the station. That way, I may justify this afternoon's excursion. ('Daytime quartets in London, Mrs Burdett?' 'Ah yes, Your Honour, but at least I billed my clients en route.')

I pull on a pair of leggings and two heavy fleeces and walk over to the barn, where Mark is painting. The ground is crunchy underfoot and the air so still that the sound of my shoes on the gravel is jarring and harsh. I stop for a bit and stand perfectly still, riveted by the sudden silence and the sense of nature – of life itself – being peacefully deferred.

The barn is so raw that inside feels colder than outside. Mark paints at the northern end of the building, where the light is right for him, his work uninterrupted by direct sun. I have entered at the south end, and though I am standing in a generous beam of silver light the illusion of warmth is just that – illusory. Church interiors always look warmer than they are, with their honey-coloured stone and stained glass in flame red and amber. Our barn is the same. I really only like it in the summer. Mark and I often discuss a better heating system for it, the one we will install when we can afford to, so he can paint in more comfort. In fact, we can just about afford it now but Mark is inexplicably resistant. I don't understand why. I've been trying to warm him up for years.

I walk around to one side of my husband so he can see me in his peripheral vision.

'Babe. I'm off.'

But Mark doesn't look up so I reach out to touch his left hand, although I don't actually touch it, I simply wait for him to register me. I spend quite a lot of my life waiting for Mark in this way, and not always because he hasn't noticed I am there. When finally he looks in my direction, I repeat myself.

'Babe, I'm off. Don't forget the fish pie, and there's plenty of veg in the fridge. Make sure the girls eat something green.'

'I'll try.'

'Don't try, succeed. They'll eat broccoli. Or just peas will do.'

'Okay.'

I look at the canvas. The work in progress is a Caribbean seascape in the early stages of a storm, a stretch of water that is quickly coming to life with undulations of aquamarine and pearl even though Mark began it only a couple of days earlier. He is working from a series of photographs that have been sent to him. Painting from static images is something he dislikes doing but that's what the client has asked for and the client is paying – handsomely, given the speed with which Mark is painting.

'It's looking good.'

'Getting there.'

I contemplate my husband. He looks and dresses as if he could rescue me if necessary. I like that. Today he is wearing a navy-blue Cornish fisherman's sweater, a thick wool scarf, a pair of old Levi's, and walking boots with thick walking socks. The blow heater to his right is on full blast but I still don't understand how his uncovered fingers remain dexterous. I work in the cold sometimes but I move around; it makes a big difference.

'It's icy in here. Surely you want some more heat.'

'You're the one that feels the chill, not me.'

'Seriously, though,' and I indicate the heater with my foot, 'we can afford to heat you better than that.'

'Not today, we can't. The repair bill for your car just arrived.'

'Ah, I missed that. What's the damage?'

'Over six hundred, plus the VAT.'

'Jesus wept! It's not even worth that any more.'

'I know. We could do with being paid on time by some of my clients.'

'Why do you never ask your agent to chase them? For heaven's sake, Mark.'

'Okay.'

'It's not okay. You're hopeless at billing people on time! I wish you'd get on top of it. It's crazy. We run overdrafts when people owe you, and then I end up ringing them for you when I have my own work to do.'

'Yeah, okay.' He frowns. 'You're looking pretty hot.'

'I'm not even dressed properly yet.'

'That's not what I meant.'

'Are you really okay about today?'

'What do you mean?'

'Well, some husbands might not like it.'

'Look,' Mark puts down his paintbrush and rummages around on the table to his right. 'I'm not "some husband". And I'm not your keeper, either. You've always been a solo operator, it's one of the things I like best about you. Just go.' He pulls a long, thin brush from a glass jar full of almost identical long, thin brushes. 'Go! I really want to get this picture cracked by the end of the week.'

Turning back to the canvas he trails the brush across a section of it, leaving a vein-blue serpentine streak in its wake. At the door, I turn back to look at him. He is up close to the canvas, squinting. 'Damn it,' he mutters, 'I really do need glasses. I can barely see what's right in front of me these days.'

Back inside the house, I take just thirteen minutes to

change and get ready; any longer than that and the preparation will be something I don't want it to be – excessive for a simple meeting of minds over music. My hair is not quite the way I like it and whilst I am irritated, a little bit of me, perversely, is glad. I do not think it right that I look my very best.

Outside once more, bag over my shoulder, car keys in my hand, the stillness is breathtaking. I glance up at the dormant trees. Everything feels suspended.

My train is late into London. I arrive at the concert hall flustered, sticky from running along Tube platforms, up escalators, and along the South Bank itself, cursing inwardly, my overcoat uncomfortably heavy, my face hot, and then suddenly – across the foyer – there he is. Wearing a long black coat, unfeasibly handsome, he is looking visibly concerned; checking his watch, scanning the small crowd, anxiously smoothing back his hair.

He catches sight of me and his relief is immediate. I can see it even now, any time I choose to recall the moment, the way his face lights up. We accelerate towards one another, kiss quickly on both cheeks, hurry into the hall as the lights go down. An usher checks the tickets Angus proffers, whispers directions to our seats. Angus says in hushed tones as we sit down, 'You look very beautiful,' and I detect in his voice a combination of pride and pleasure, as if I am ratifying some choice he made earlier. I whisper in return, 'I look very dishevelled.' He murmurs, 'I was honestly beginning to think you might not turn up,' and I can feel his breath in my ear.

I try to concentrate on the music but you really do need to be in the mood for Beethoven quartets and I am not. I'm not crazy about Beethoven at the best of times. I know he's a genius but he's a fractious genius and he makes me feel jittery. He certainly requires more attention than I can muster with Angus sitting beside me to my left, with his hands on his thighs – large hands, strong hands, the fingers splayed. If he stirs even slightly I feel myself prickle, and I am aware of my body's slight but deliberate incline away from his: I am conscious of my legs, shoulders, hands, of where they are and how they might look; conscious especially of my eyes cast towards Angus, downwards and to the left – a thief's angle, eyeing up the goods. I risk a slow, sly glimpse of his profile. I can smell him. I don't recognize his after-shave but I wouldn't; I know only Mark's and this is not it. Angus's scent is sharp and imposing. It is not, I think suddenly, the scent of a virtuous man. It is too impeccable.

There is no interval and therefore no let-up, so a couple of quartets later we emerge on to the South Bank without preamble and I am disconcerted at being out here all of a sudden, feeling edgy, taut and excited. I have heard almost nothing of the music and Angus and I have barely had five minutes to speak and yet here we are walking side by side, and he has turned to me and smiled five, no, more like ten, times already. The temperature has dropped. The cold is no longer invigorating: the sky has clouded over and a fresh wind reports its easterly influence in surprising, bitter stabs. Now, I am as grateful to be well wrapped in my layers as I was frustrated earlier, in my haste to reach Angus.

Angus on the South Bank: a man inviting description. His overcoat is so long, and so wide at the hem, it could pass as a cloak. I am enthralled by the garment's low-pitched ostentation, by the way it concedes to him, simultaneously obeying and accentuating his body's movements; and I am impressed, too, by the drama of a hemline few straight men would wish to entertain. There is a flourish to Angus's gait, a fluency exacerbated by the coat that is redolent of a conductor's swagger. Momentarily, I picture my children on Bonfire Night – frenzied little conductors themselves – assuming exaggerated gestures as they write their names with sparklers, making letters that dissipate the second they become apparent: gold script fizzing in the obsidian air, its beauty as fleeting as musical notes. And as my thoughts come full circle, it strikes me that with his leonine hair and commanding presence Angus looks like the conductor of an orchestra himself, someone to whom fifty people would surrender in unison without question – which amuses me because my brother Ed, who really is one, with the Berlin Philharmonic, has the permanently strained and slightly derelict appearance of an exhausted commuter.

I consider the theatricality of Angus's demeanour, a theatricality he seems completely to possess, and I see that this way of being in his own body, this easy flamboyance, is probably something he has cultivated over a lifetime and come to recognize as a great advantage, for it will have made him impossible to disregard. It only takes a walk beside a person to see these things, sometimes.

'How tall are you?'

'Six foot three, or thereabouts.'

'Or thereabouts.' I smile. 'Men always do that. My husband is convinced he's six foot two. He's not.'

'So, he's shorter than me?'

'That's not the point. The point is, you're not six foot three – I don't believe.'

'I'm a man,' Angus shrugs, apologetically. 'Men argue every last half-inch.'

'Which is ridiculous.'

'Because women don't care?'

'Oh, women do.'

He nods slowly, taking me in.

I smile; a Cheshire cat smile, damn it. I can feel it.

We duck out of the wind and into a cafe: it is Angus's

suggestion. 'It'll be quieter elsewhere,' he had said, when proposing a hot drink as we dithered in the concert hall foyer once the recital had concluded. Now, he puts his arm around me, not quite touching me, just carving a shape around my shoulders as he guides me ahead of him through the door, saying, 'Are you sure this is okay? There are one or two other places further along but they're all much of a muchness.'

It's warm. The seats look reasonably comfy. I tell him it's perfect.

On the walls are old, laminated posters advertising plays at the National Theatre: sweat-browed actors with contorted expressions are frozen in poses suggesting pain, passion, emergency. Love and war. Under a long glass canopy running counter to the messages of turmoil above is a soothing selection of flapjacks, muffins and cheesecakes. Further along the wall, the cast of *Guys and Dolls* is belting its collective heart out above an espresso machine.

We order a large pot of tea, a round of cheese toast to share and two warm, dark chocolate brownies, oozing like unset tarmac.

'I love to eat,' says Angus, with relish.

'Me too.'

At a table by the window the afternoon slides away like the river running parallel to us, through the glass. We talk a bit about music, much more about ourselves. I keep my coat around my shoulders for I am shivering from the inside out and cannot stop, but Angus has removed his cloak. It lies over the back of the chair beside him but even inert it embodies prospect, of being filled by Angus. Angus's eyes are brown, his hair thick and his skin olive, like a Latin.

'Actually, I'm as English as they come,' he tells me, when I ask about his forename, 'but my paternal grandfather was Scottish, and my mother spent her childhood holidays in Scotland and loved it there.'

'Thus Angus?'

'Thus Angus.'

He asks me lots of questions. I sermonize about Mark and the children. He wants to know what makes me tick. I pay tribute to marriage and family life. He says he means, 'What makes you tick, apart from that?' and I realize it is a very long time since anyone asked me that question and how it feels similar to being handed a beautifully wrapped present when it's not your birthday. I volley carefully with return questions of my own but Angus is determined and his enquiries become steadily more insistent. He wants to hear and I am conscious of wanting to be heard. He seeks confidences: I hedge but insinuate promise. I don't stop to wonder whether I should be behaving this way; it seems oddly admissible, given the circumstances. Besides which, it is interesting to do, to flex old muscles in a game of this sort. Years ago, I knew how to catch a man across a room or a table and though I say it myself, I was good at it. I assumed I had forgotten how. It seems not.

All the same, I am ashamed by how much I am prepared so readily to share. It's not the content of my disclosures that offends me – for when it comes to facts, I reveal little – so much as their indulgent manner. I haven't had this kind of conversation with a man since I was in my early twenties and exhilarating though it was to get what I wanted, I was still appalled by the indecent ease with which I could accelerate in a flash from straightforward to siren. And yet it seems that this is exactly what I am doing right now, quite suddenly at a point in my life when everything I ever wanted I already have, at home. It feels like an unexpected detour into old rooms and former lives, or into a cupboard in which I discover that a long-discarded costume still fits and an earlier version of myself is around after all. It is a huge surprise, a jolt both fantastic and preposterous, but except for the sharp stimulant to my vanity it is surely meaningless. At least, that is what I try to tell myself, as far as it is possible with Angus sitting only inches away. It's all very well being adorned quite suddenly in some historic version of oneself but to what end? Raiments from the past are just that: past.

I remember one of my mother's general guidelines for life: 'Do not, in the first place, put yourself in a position from which you may later need to extricate yourself.' Given my mother's contained and close-fitting character, it was a maxim I always interpreted as meaning, 'Take no risks,' so I ignored it. Even a moderate chance of a poor outcome never struck me as a sufficient reason not to try something new, and accustomed as I was, when younger, to seeking excitement with the dedication I later applied to maintaining domestic security, my mother's dictum seemed to me not only unrealistic but irrelevant – even absurd – considering the kind of person I was. If having an adventure involved hazard and exposure, and opting for defiance over caution meant that something interesting, unusual or even incredible might happen, then so be it.

As I got older, however, I came to see that that is not what my mother was trying to impart; that her emphasis was instead on the safeguarding of oneself from unnecessary future difficulties. If she was advising me to keep more than half an eye on my general conduct and reputation, and above all to avoid those situations in which I might set myself up for embarrassment or unwelcome obligation, then sitting here today with Angus, I can see her point.

The cafe has filled up. People are coming in cold, wanting hot food. Angus pours tea from a second pot, which he had to queue for some time to get. While he did, I savoured him from behind.

'Your husband,' Angus says carefully, 'sounds like a truly amazing man.'

'He's the love of my life. With the children, of course.'

'I wouldn't know what that feels like.' Angus sighs. 'Never married. No kids.'

'Your choice, no doubt.'

'Yes.'

'Right. So, don't pull that sighing number with me.'

Angus looks me straight in the eye. I don't flinch.

'Wow!' His tone is one of awe, and something else, too – a relish akin to delight. 'You really do tell it like it is.'

'I'm sorry, that was awful of me. I've never been much of a diplomat.'

'Don't be sorry. I appreciate straight talk.'

I should be mortified. I have, with minimal knowledge of this man and certainly no right to tell him what I think of him, been harsh and provocative. But I am not mortified and neither is he. He is charmed. I suspected he would be and am glad my instincts served me well; it is pleasing to be reminded that the way to another person is sometimes so easy, and the route so clear.

Now he leans forwards, his arms stretched partway across the table, and he settles himself purposefully. He looks as if he is bedding down finally into something he has been hoping for.

'Right,' he says. 'Your turn. Shoot.'

I take a deep breath.

'Okay then, Mr Wilson, a straight question: what about your amazing woman?'

He does not miss a beat.

'There is no amazing woman.'

When I exhale, I realize I have been holding my breath.

'Surely there are some hopeful birds out there?'

'Not that I'm interested in.'

'There must be one or two lurkers.'

'Lurkers!' He throws back his head and laughs with such vivacity that I think, *So this is what you look like.*

I laugh, too.

'I have no lurkers, sweetheart.'

I don't believe him, a man this attractive.

'Lurkers!' he repeats. 'You really are funny.'

He gives me a long, quizzical look, which I return. If he thinks he can outstare me he's mistaken. I'm married to a lip-reader: I am considerably less discomfited than most people by a locked gaze.

'Okay,' he concedes, 'I might have the odd lurker. And no, they are not my students. But,' and he lingers for a few seconds, enjoying himself or my anticipation, or very likely both, 'there is not one I would want to be sitting at this table right now. To put it bluntly,' his expression grows more serious, 'there is only one person I want sitting opposite me right now. And she is.'

A woman squeezes past our table and accidentally

catches the end of a teaspoon with her bag. It falls to the floor, together with a paper napkin. She doesn't notice. Neither Angus nor I move to pick it up.

'You must know,' I say soberly, and I want to sound steadfast and dependable, 'I've never so much as glanced left or right. Not once, in all the time I've known Mark.'

Angus stretches his right hand across the table, closer to mine. In a raised vein between the second and third fingers, a soft pulse is visible.

'So, I'm quite safe, then.' His voice has dropped to a near-whisper.

The wish to stroke that raised vein is upsetting me.

'You definitely are. You're a one-off music date.'

'That, if I may say so, is a disappointment.'

I want to feel that vein. I want his pulse under my fingers.

The cafe door is being held open for a woman with a pram and the draught from outside is savage. My head buzzes. The clatter of crockery, voices and scraped chairs ebbs and flows around us, yet everything seems suddenly to close in and the light to fail. Angus's hand is closer still to mine and now he reaches for my uncurling fingers and they meet – his index finger and mine, just the tips – and while we contemplate them, very quietly Angus says, 'Lucy, tell me about you before Mark. When you were growing up, what were you like?'

Transfixed by the pressure of Angus's finger, I cannot meet his eye.

'In what sense?'

'Any sense,' he replies, and his voice is close, closer. 'All senses. Tell me,' he croons. 'Tell me all about you.'

I look up and away.

'I was not at ease.'

'Why? Living with your famously difficult famous dad?'

'Partly. I was just not a relaxed person and I think that's probably still true. I mean, it's different with the children, with them I'm someone else entirely, but I've never been especially contented and that has probably made me restless and with Mark . . . I mean, I'm not –'

'Not what?'

I consider how truthful I am prepared to be.

'I'm just not an easy person.'

'How so?'

We regard each other for a long time and what might have been a plain, wordless interval between us amplifies into a fecund silence from which deliverance feels both urgent and impossible. Finally, Angus places his finger on top of mine and presses its firm, warm pad upon my glossed pink nail.

'Tell me,' he insists. 'I want to hear.'

'It's hard to say.'

'Lucy,' he says. 'Look at me.'

'Okay. I'm looking.'

'Why are you not happy?'

It's a dance and we both know the steps.

Angus walks me to the Tube, to the top of the steps that disappear underground. We stand in the dingy remnants of the day's light and the wind that is blowing even harder than it was earlier. I am shivering still, and not just from the cold.

'Well,' I say, 'this is me.'

'And this is me, wishing that you weren't going home.' He smiles ruefully. 'I hope you'll come again soon – to London, I mean.'

'I do from time to time. I've got some friends here.'

'Perhaps you might add me to their number.'

'I might well.'

He laughs. It's infectious and I giggle.

'That's more like it!'

We kiss on both cheeks; a brief and faultless conclusion.

'Angus, I really must go otherwise my train will turn into a pumpkin.'

A strand of hair whips across my face. Angus lifts it carefully to one side and loops it over my ear. Immediately, the wind blows it across once more and quickly I brush it aside myself, turning away from him.

'Go on, then,' he urges, as I run down the first few steps into a blast of stale, warm air. 'Make haste, Cinderella!'

I stop and look back up. Angus is smiling and waving, and without even thinking, I do it; I take off one shoe. Wobbling slightly on my other, still shod, foot, I place the shoe on the step beside me. A woman hurries past, huffing forcefully: I am in her way. A man dithers on the step above mine, confused. When he realizes that I am going nowhere, he dodges around me, irritated. At the top of the steps Angus is curious. I pick up the shoe and wave it at him and when I see realization dawn upon him at last, clumsily I pull it back on, and I smile.

'I would have brought it to you!' he calls.

I know you would.

'I could have put it on for you!'

And it would fit.

'Mummy! You're back!'

Melanie emerges into the half-light of the hall. She is wearing pyjamas patterned with jungle animals and she has a half-eaten chocolate biscuit in one hand.

'Hello, Mel! Gorgeous girl!'

She hurls herself at me. I squeeze her tightly, growl, snap at her fingers and the biscuit. Delighted, she shrieks and wriggles. I squeeze her harder, growl more fiercely and snap again at the biscuit, which she stuffs into her mouth. I feign shock. Through giggles compromised by crumbs and saliva she munches hard, swallows, then winds her arms around my hips and pushes her head against my stomach. I thread my fingers into her hair.

'My beautiful baby.'

My phone pings.

'Where's your sister?'

'In the kitchen with Daddy.'

'You girls should be asleep. It's way after your bedtime.'

'Daddy says it's okay to wait for you.'

'Daddy would say that.'

Again, the phone pings. I pull away slightly from Mel, swipe the screen, read the text message above her, my wrist resting lightly on her head: '*Thank you so much for such a special afternoon. What a pity Cinderella had to go – the conversation had only just begun. Hope you returned safely to your crew. A. X*'

The hall is gloomy and the phone screen bright. Illuminated, I reply politely to Angus, and in the time it takes me to divest myself of my daughter, keys, bag, coat and scarf, Angus has texted back: '*Next time, I could cook you a proper meal at home (if you would like). A. X*'

Quickly, I write: '*I would like. L x*'

'Mummy!' Mel is tugging at me, willing me further into the house.

In the kitchen, Mark and Miranda are bent over a mixing bowl. Miranda has a wooden spoon in one hand. There is flour and cocoa dust all over the work surfaces and smears of butter on the handle of the cold tap. An empty packet of chocolate buttons and some daisy-patterned cake cases are to one side. The oven is on. It is eight-thirty and a school night and the place is a mess. It is proof, if any were needed, that there really is no such thing as a free lunch. I anticipate the clean-up ahead, which moral imperative demands that I do.

'Hey there,' says Mark. 'Good day?'

Once more, the phone pings. Mark is oblivious to the sound itself but not my reaction to it.

'Yes, thanks.' I swipe the screen. 'Sorry, just a sec.'

'Who's that?'

'Angus. Making sure I got back safely.'

'How solicitous of him.'

'Don't be daft.'

I read the message.

'You would? Lovely, Lucy! Or do I mean "Lovely Lucy . . ."? I think I might mean both. A. XX'

My name is not Lucy, not really. I'm glad about this because the name Lucy is quintessentially English, and as I have no English blood I feel no kinship with it: it suggests to me an aspect of the English character that I do not feel I possess, a kind of uptight restraint masked by good manners. It's difficult to pin down but the kind of person called Lucy represents, to me, someone whose feelings are stifled and internalized, a person with a resistance to joy – and I know that's utterly ridiculous and there must be plenty of joyful Lucys out there but I haven't met one. The ones I know are careful and impassive and I cannot imagine error in their lives. I can't envisage them muddy, or distrait, or in the sack, and for those reasons alone I don't identify with them. That could be because the three Lucys I know are all friends of my mother's and each of them makes me feel inadequate. They're hard to fault and I really don't like that in a person. I prefer people with their flaws on the outside, like mine.

I ran this entire 'Lucy' theory past Mark once but all he said was, 'Babe, you seriously need to get out more.'

My real name is Lucia, after my father's mother, who was Italian, but early on my French mother called me Lucy, and it stuck. It was so simple and yet so transforming an amendment, the switch in infancy from a touch of Mediterranean exotica to upright Englishness via a few vowels – an Englishness that even my mother's tendency to pronounce my name with a Gallic swing upwards on the second syllable would fail to mitigate. Attempts during my teens to persuade my family to stick

27

to the original appellation failed. Whenever I asked them to call me Lucia they didn't, I guess because they were used to Lucy by then and they're anyway not the most amenable bunch of people.

My father's father was Welsh, and while it's a pretty combustible mix, Welsh and Italian, it always struck me as oddly symmetrical, given that the Welsh – being every bit as impassioned as the Italians – are basically Italians turned inside out. Their emotions, instead of burning flamboyantly bright on the surface, smoulder beneath it, and their unyielding Celtic disposition perfectly mirrors its opposite – the famous Latin appetite for volcanic bust-ups and reconciliations.

In keeping with his contrary genetic inheritance, my father has a predisposition for both sudden outbursts and morose silences, and though he has calmed down a bit since I was small, his liking for a colourful scrap far exceeds the enthusiasm most people have for disagreements. Spirited discourse is meat and drink to him; at mealtimes especially, arguing the toss with friends and colleagues, his appetite is for blood. Yet when depression settles upon him he is possessed instead by an austere brooding, which perhaps appropriately he takes himself to Wales to indulge in – sometimes for weeks on end – staying in a cousin's cottage on the Ceredigion coast where in contrast to his sociable life at home with my mother he sees and speaks to no one. Sometimes there is a television series, the writing of which he must complete, to provide some broad explanation to others for his long absences but in the family, for as long as I can remember, the cousin's seaboard cottage in Wales has been referred to with casual irreverence as 'the sulking house'.

During my teens, all my school friends wanted to meet my dad. He was the high point of their first visits to our house. He knew it, too, and had perfected the blend of implied intimacy and remoteness that so mesmerizes people, particularly susceptible females: 'Oh, how lovely to meet you at last, I've heard so much about you from Lucy.' And as my friends fidgeted with thrilled self-consciousness, he would retreat to his study and close the door firmly behind him with a flourish. That way, his absence might be felt immediately and his magic – now just out of reach – seem all the more beguiling.

Dazzled, they would chime, 'Wow, your dad is so nice! So down to earth!'

Down to earth: such a meaningless phrase. It's not one I would ever use, particularly with reference to my dad. But I gave up contesting it – and all the straightforward-ness it implies – because when your father's a popular TV historian, his easy captivation of others with the orna-ment of BBC fame means there's simply no point.

'Yeah,' I'd concede. 'He's okay.'

If it was a demanding business growing up with John Parry-Jones for a father, my mother, Hélène, compensated for it with a more relaxed attitude. Put bluntly, she combined full-time scientific research with ice-cool rationale and near-indifference to family life or discord. What this meant in practical terms is that she was seldom on our case, or not overtly so. I don't doubt that she cared about my brother Ed and me but she loved my father above all else and although her feelings for her children were steadfast they showed themselves in a manner that could at best be described as hands-off and at worst neglectful. The fact that she was rarely at home, never cooked and barely noticed what time we went to bed (and from our mid-teens onwards, with whom), was altogether in keeping with her particular brand of maternal care – which was to care much less than most mothers about everything, leaving us to figure things out for ourselves and run our lives in parallel with hers, alongside but not overlapping.

Since becoming a mother myself I've tried to convince myself that at least my own mother knew her strengths (epidemiology) and her weaknesses (family life). I've told myself it was just as well she had the good sense to concentrate on the former and delegate the latter to a woman called Margie who came in on weekdays to neaten up the edges of our lives and make sure that Ed and I had something hot to eat for supper whilst our parents were eating out with other, more interesting people than us. 'What delights did Margie produce for you today?' my mother would ask, long after our supper had been cleared, and 'Margie's delights' soon became a family shorthand for golden-topped nursery food like shepherd's pie, toad-in-the-hole and apple crumble. Actually, I say Margie neatened up the edges of our lives but really the opposite was true: she was central to everything. Family life without her would have fallen apart like the walls of a building collapsing outwards, leaving us all exposed, not just to the chill outside but to one another, gathered together, bewildered.

My friends, however, thought my mother was incredibly cool. They envied me her tight black jeans, laissez-faire attitude and general abstraction. They didn't know about the slight shiver that went down my spine when she came home. They wouldn't have guessed that I wondered what I meant to her, and that my relationship with her was subject to persistent insecurity. It's such a trivial example when I could produce a hundred others but when she walked through the door at the end of her day, the simple greeting, 'Hello, Lucy,' really riled me because it was not simple at all. It was in fact, 'Hello? Lucy?' – and given that she was already in the room with me it's not as if I could have been Dad or Ed. And it may not sound like much, and I know the French like to sing-song their way to the end of a sentence, but that bloody question mark over my presence got right under my skin. It made me feel like an unexpected visitor to the household instead of my mother's resident daughter, the one who was there when she left at breakfast-time dressed all in black, her lipstick pale pink, her coffee-coloured hair swept up into a coil and detained with a tortoiseshell pin; immaculate despite herself.

'Hello? Lucy?'

'That's me.'

'Productive day?'

'It was okay. Jed's coming around later.'

'*Bien*. Which one's Jed, again?'

'Mum, you know who Jed is.'

Standing in the kitchen, rifling through the papers in her briefcase, she muttered through a thick strand of hair that had escaped the tortoiseshell pin and was now falling in a perfect curve across her face, 'He's the blonde one?'

'Yes,' I sighed.

She looked relieved, like a child who has taken a wild stab at an answer in class and got it right.

'Ah yes, of course. He is with Amanda, *non*?'

'*Oui.*'

'She has finesse, Amanda. *Delicatesse.*'

And then, nodding in the direction of my father's study, towards which she was already heading, she said, 'Now, where is my husband skulking? That's the really important question.'

* * *

Until I was nearly eleven, the village school nearby provided respite from family life. We planted water-cress, tended hamsters and dug up earthworms. The atmosphere was festive and the headmistress a person so given to spontaneity that on hot summer afternoons she would sometimes cancel lessons in favour of trips to the river, where we would have water fights in its pebbly shallows. 'Try that now,' she said drily, years later when we ran into one another in the street, 'and you'd be strung up.'

The fun was not to last. Shortly before my eleventh birthday, my father got the bit between his teeth about the co-educational boarding school where my brother was excelling and I found myself on a taster weekend there. My experience of the first morning, subgrouped together with seven potential fellow pupils, was enough for me to know what I couldn't take. The girls tossed their hair and eyed one another suspiciously; the boys used phrases like, 'I beg to differ,' and, 'In my humble opinion.' One girl had a mother who was involved in the Middle East peace talks, another a thirteen-year-old sister who was writing a musical (allegedly). I did the only logical thing. I sprinted to the railway station just under half a mile away and with some pocket money I had stowed in the bottom of my bag for emergencies, bought myself a single fare. Bound for home I cowered in my seat, glaring out of the window. When the train arrived, I phoned my parents from a telephone box on the platform, my hands shaking so much I could hardly push the coins into the slot.

'Please can you come and get me?' I quavered. 'I'm at the station.'

'You are where?!'

Around the kitchen table that evening my father groaned irritably and demanded, 'So what do you expect us to do?'

I asked what was wrong with the local secondary school: all my friends from primary school were going there. My father shuddered like a man contemplating a treacherous pass across a deep ravine and said, 'Oxbridge! Chances from there are slim.' I said that even if I got into Oxford or Cambridge – and that was unlikely – I wouldn't want to go anyway. I told him wild horses wouldn't drag me. I said, 'I don't want to be like all the people who come to our house.'

'What did you say?!'

'I don't want to be that kind of person!' I spluttered. 'They think they know everything! They think being clever makes them better than everyone else. It's horrible.'

My father's mouth fell open. Mine was dry with fear.

'How dare you!' he exclaimed. 'You're ten years old, damn it!'

'Nearly eleven!'

'You're a juvenile! You have some of the best thinkers in

this country in and out of your home on a weekly basis and you have the audacity to say—'

'I hate them! And I hate you! I don't belong here. I don't belong anywhere!'

My father's eyes blazed. I felt a familiar panic rise in my gut.

I wondered then whether he might actually slap me: he never had before but I feared it nonetheless, the physical expulsion of my father's rage. I had witnessed it often enough. He thumped the living daylights out of tables, kicked doors, slammed his clenched fist against walls, raving and ungovernable, breathing hard, spitting, 'Fuuuuuuck!' through gritted teeth and a mist of saliva. Instead, this time, he snarled, 'Then you're even more of a damn fool than I thought you were this morning!' and stormed out of the room, casting his chair aside so violently that it cracked against the dresser and fell over.

My mother and I stared at one another across the kitchen table for a bit before she sat up straight, put her hands on her thighs, and in a moment of exceptional ordinariness said, '*Voilà*. I'll make us some scrambled eggs.'

This uncommon treat augured well. A couple of days later she announced over breakfast that there was nothing wrong with the local school and I could go there if I wanted to. My father said, 'Oh, for God's sake, Hélène, they don't even do Latin!' to which my mother responded, 'We can always pay for extra tuition.'

'Latin?!' I wailed. 'Please, no.'

'What's the point,' my father growled, 'of sending her locally when a first-rate school would deliver the whole bang shoot?'

'John.' My mother's tone was imperturbable, reasonable: she rarely resorts to out-and-out condescension although one always feels it lurking within close range. 'You argue in public for state education and yet when it comes to your own children you lose your nerve. Hypocrite! *Faux-jeton!*'

But my father was in no mood for dialogue. Black Dog was not far away. We had become adept at sensing this familiar interloper, knowing intuitively when he was prowling around the suburbs of my father's mind, ready any minute to break in and take possession of the centre for days, weeks. Black Dog dulled my sparky dad: he claimed a clever, imposing person and drained his thinking dry, stripped it of colour and surprise, muffled his speech, killed his artful humour, reduced him to something rudimentary, brutish.

Sweeping aside the newspaper and a plate of unfinished toast, my father declared the discussion a waste of time and immaterial to the purpose, which was to get me into a good school. He leaned across the table and got right up close to my mother's face when he said this; too close, I thought.

'Dad!' I cried out. 'Don't!'

'John!' my mother intervened, sharply. *'Ça suffit! Enough!'*

My mother proved victorious. She waited another day or two until the heat in him had diminished, registered me for the local school and left it at that. My father said the whole thing would be an unmitigated disaster.

It wasn't. I did what I had to do and at the end of it all I was offered a place at Swansea to read English. I'd chosen Swansea not for its tenuous family connection but because it was coastal, and I love the sea: it seemed a pretty sound basis for a decision about where to spend my first three years away from the suppression of home. My father choked on his coffee when I told him my plans. He had little affinity with his Welsh background, even though it had its political advantages for a left-wing historian. He barely spoke to me during my first term at university except occasionally to demand on the phone, 'My dear girl, if you had to go west, why the hell not Bristol, at least?'

In Swansea, I learned to surf, withstood a year of Chaucer and twentieth-century semiotics and by then, by God, I was fed up. So were the tutors and not just with me. Decades of unventilated debate had left most of them near-suffocated. Gasping for air myself, I left and got a job serving meals in a pub on the bay where by chance I ran into an old school friend who had spent the previous winter working a ski season in the Dolomites while I was contending with the spectacular insularity of Roland Barthes and the tedious specifics of Middle English.

I wasted no more time, though my father would argue that that is precisely what I did. Waitressing, cleaning, childminding, teaching English, fruit-picking: it didn't matter to me what it was, as long as I could raise the air fare behind a bar in the UK to travel repeatedly as far away as possible. Cairo, Bombay, Tel Aviv, Harare: my mother says she lost a lifetime of sleep over my choice of world capitals – an admission of maternal concern so uncharacteristic that it made those places even more exciting in retrospect. The toughest and most demoralizing job of all (apart from harvesting peanuts on a farm near the Gaza Strip – the leaves of the plants brought me out in a vivid, prickly rash) was hosing down the stinking, blackened walls of a rubber factory outside Tel Aviv, for eight hours a day. The work was physically relentless, and so noisy and solitary that conversation of any kind was impossible. After just six days I walked out and never went back. The only other job that came close to the rubber factory for isolation was a short stint in Ireland as a live-in au pair for a couple who ran an IT company from a bleak farmhouse in County Westmeath – surely the one bit of Irish landscape its venerated God had overlooked. The place was flat and dreary and the nearest town miles away; plus, the children were too small to commune with and their parents constantly off in Dublin.

In contrast, by far the easiest gig – the only peril was to oversleep – was raking the sand at sunrise on a quiet beach that fronted a scruffy B&B in Grand Bahama, before serving breakfast to affable, retired couples from Florida, and the odd honeymooning pair. The place was managed by a large, shifty American guy whom I was certain ran drugs from Miami, and his curiously buttoned-up English wife. They were the strangest couple. He scarcely spoke and was not often about. When he was, he ambled around the terrace in a baseball cap and large baggy shorts with *Palm Beach Cardinals* printed down the side of one leg. She wore Laura Ashley dresses that bore comparison with Edwardian smocks, and her hair in a pinned-up style that I guessed had not altered in years. They had no children. It pretty much concluded my wanderings, that job, and whilst it was a relief from the smog, poverty and precarious political situations of the East and Middle East, I was bored out of my mind after a fortnight. I stayed a couple of months. I had no other plans and the diving was pretty good.

In London, in the flat I shared with two old school friends who had proper jobs with moral purpose (trainee teacher, trainee physiotherapist), the bookshelves in my tiny room were covered with the totems of my travels: wooden bowls, pottery, seashells, pebbles, small carved animals, and sticks stroked smooth by the oceans. On my return from Harare I removed some bookshelves altogether to make room for my photographs. Space was tight, I wanted visual inspiration, so some literature had to go. Twentieth-century authors survived the transition but Jane Austen and her ilk were relocated to Oxfam. My rebellion was complete.

Disappointment comes in many forms. My loose-fitting life with its ill-defined perimeters did little for my parents. I stretched their comprehension to its limits. They were exasperated by the walls that no longer displayed rows of orange-spined Penguin paperbacks but instead, in A4 clip-frames from WHSmith, images of pearl-toothed Zimbabwean toddlers, the pyramids at Giza, and a pleasing range of Middle Eastern sunsets. My parents saw no potential for intellectual satisfaction in the arenas that I chose and little to justify what seemed to them a promiscuous attitude to culture in general. That I could reside briefly in Bombay and learn no Hindi bewildered my mother, especially. I was only there for four months, working mainly with a bunch of Australian rugby jocks and Dutch primary school teachers – the latter group spoke perfect English – but she was unconvinced. My tendency to hop from one place to another, investing in each no more than temporary interest, was about as close to whoring as she could imagine, only more demeaning.

In our family, foreign excursions came with the territory that was my parents' lot: public appearances, talks and conferences took them to the furthest reaches of a number of university campuses and as children, my brother and I sometimes went, too. We were invited to eat home-made ice cream with a history professor at Harvard, offered a bumpy ride across Sydney Harbour in a speedboat owned by the Director General of the Australian Broadcasting Corporation and permitted to stroke the husky dogs in Tromsø that belonged to the only doctor in the Arctic Circle with a special interest in tropical medicine. That my own progress across continents should be motivated by neither academic pursuit nor pilgrim intent but instead be a means to an end in itself, my parents simply did not understand.

'Peripatetic,' I once said to my father, 'that's all I am. Nothing wrong with that.'

'There's plenty wrong with it,' he replied, 'including the fact that peripatetic implies a certain nomadic grandeur, or at least a vague sense of purpose. Itinerant is I think the word you want.'

'Tramp' came to mind. I thought about my backpack, of which I was proud. Battle-scarred, it had been crushed beneath the wheels of a bus in Victoria Falls and stained by stray splatters of engine oil when strapped to the rear of a sputtering 1972 Enfield Bullet on which I hitched a lift to Varanasi with a gay nurse from Auckland, named Ron; a nice guy.

Stung, I retorted, 'Okay then, so how about "drifter"? "Wanderer"?'

'They'll do, too,' my father remarked, vaguely. 'By the way,' he continued, jabbing at the paper in front of him, 'when did you last read anything worthwhile?'

I stared at him. Perusing the *London Review of Books* over his little frameless glasses his nose was wrinkled as if he were taking issue not only with me but with the premise of the article he was reading. His hair was tousled and sun-streaked and his arms brown: he was still in his tennis gear from early that morning. 'Prof Hollywood', they call him at the university – not on account of his TV films but his appearance. He looks like Robert Redford.

Sod you, I thought. I love my dad, but still.

My mother for a change put to one side her concerns about my lazy mind and lack of ambition and was merely relieved I wasn't raped or murdered. I was robbed, three times to be precise, and found myself in plenty of dodgy situations with men but they were par for the course and mostly easy to handle. Only once did I wonder earnestly whether I would successfully exit a car unharmed by its two male occupants. Yet while she remained unaware of the genuine dangers I had permitted myself, my mother was as disappointed as my father by my repudiation of a livelihood – any livelihood – they thought worth writing home about.

Meanwhile, my brother Ed charted with care and purpose his route to distinction in a single, hard discipline. Decorated with prizes and plaudits, including gold-dust student placements in Tokyo and Berlin, he was mentored by Vladimir Ashkenazy and – in the very same month that I secured a summer job making cheese-and-ham toasties in the Penzance Lido Snack Shack – invited to conduct the London Symphony Orchestra for the first time, aged only twenty-five.

By the time I was twenty-five myself, defending the liberty of a baseless and impecunious lifestyle had worn thin. I fancied myself as a travel photographer but floating around with a camera was lonely and I knew the way forward financially was more likely the recording of local weddings and children's portraits than colourful Eastern spice markets. I longed for an anchor and knew that I needed to tether myself to something solid: my friends were all toiling or roosting. Un-garlanded, I was an embarrassment to my parents. Until, that is, aged twenty-six, I became engaged to Mark. Only then was I released from the pressure to prove myself. My own shortcomings were no less extant but in my parents' eyes they were moderated by my future husband's excellence. I had

43

wound up with a man of calibre. I wondered whether to feel relieved.

'My home,' says Angus, as I stand and look around me.

'What's it like?' I had written in an email. *'I'm fascinated.'*

'It's not a narrow-boat like the ones you see on the canals, it's a former Dutch timber barge. It's no beauty on the outside but it's pretty big, with two proper storeys – it's about 1,000 square feet which is more than enough for me. I bought it in the seventies as a shell because it was dirt-cheap and I rebuilt it with a couple of mates, which is why it's a bit of a hotchpotch. It's all changed along here since then. It had a lovely, artsy vibe when I was younger but now it's sadly rather smart and wealthy (neither of which I am!), though you still can't beat the view of the river. But why don't you come and see for yourself? Houseboat Verity, Cheyne Walk, Chelsea, sw10.'

Before me is an open-plan, blonde interior of pale walls, flaxen sofa, creamy floorboards and glass tables. It has the unifying pallor of a place suggestive of life but not properly inhabited and quite suddenly a 1970s hotel suite in a James Bond film springs to mind; I am half-expecting a shagpile carpet. Angus's home, with its soft, light appearance, seems somewhat incompatible with its imposing, charcoal-maned occupant.

But then, like a mist lifting over a town to reveal the edges of buildings and trees, details come gradually into sharp relief. The shock of the new – the shock of being here at all – has temporarily blinded me to the long row of bookshelves all the way up and along one wall. Hardbacks, paperbacks and music scores are clearly divided but jammed together or piled on top of one another horizontally where space has become tight. A separate section of the shelves, with specially designed, small compartments, is crammed with CDs, many hundreds – no, more like thousands – of them.

At the end of the room, in front of a huge picture window, is a Steinway grand piano in toffee-coloured wood, the Thames its backdrop. The piano lid is halfway up. Three modern landscape paintings in oil (two of them are on the slant, I notice, wishing immediately to correct their angles) are on the wall opposite, interspersed by some etchings; and an inundation of wool blankets in deep reds and blues – Scottish wool perhaps, or Welsh – spill from a large wicker basket on the floor at one end of the sofa. The rug behind the sofa, that abuts the long windows at the boat's prow, is Persian, with borders and motifs in sapphire and scarlet, and in all of it I see what I missed at first: the joyous colour and mild disarray of a life in process.

'Oh, it's amazing.'

'I am so glad you like it!' Angus's eyes crinkle with

pleasure. 'It's me, really, this place. I've been here all my life; well, all my adult life, anyway.'

His hands are stuffed deep into the pockets of a navy-blue-and-grey-speckled cardigan: it's baggy and the wool is thick and coarse; it has a Nordic air about it. Now, in a broad gesture that embraces this marine home of his, Angus stretches his arms out wide so that the cardigan momentarily becomes wings. Beneath the cardigan wings is a blue cotton shirt with a subtle flowery pattern and beneath that a pair of dark blue cords with an attractive plain brown leather belt. I imagine a moment of undoing.

'My darling,' he says, 'let me take your coat.'

My darling.

'Thank you.'

He moves behind me and my overcoat slides into his waiting hands.

'You look wonderful,' he says.

I am wearing a short dark green skirt, a white shirt and long, black boots. A substantial gold rope chain that once belonged to Mark's mother Jane is around my neck and a heavy gold bangle that Mark gave me on our first wedding anniversary is on my left wrist. I would be lying if I said that – this time – I had given my appearance little thought. My mother used to do that and it was annoying: I remember thinking that the least she could do was admit to the trouble she took.

By the front door, where assorted jackets hang, and shoes are lined in rows, Angus places my coat on a chunky wooden peg. I notice the highly polished, black slip-on boots, the heavy winter lace-ups and two pairs of beaten-up deck shoes, those slip-ons that are really plain old moccasins but with a name to suggest place and purpose, and with it the implication that you will never slip and break your ankle on deck with these on your feet. And maybe you won't, although presumably the real point is this: you have the shoes, you have the boat, you are a dude.

A phone rings, its sound muffled.

'Damn,' says Angus, hesitating.

'It's no problem. Answer it.'

'It can wait. You said this would be a flying visit. I mustn't waste a second of you.'

'I shan't disappear while you take a call. Please do.'

'Okay.' He rummages in his trouser pocket, pulls out his mobile. 'Hello? Ah Richard, hello! Can you hang on a second? I have a friend visiting.'

He covers the phone with his hand. 'Actually, I probably should deal with this if you honestly don't mind? I'm so sorry. I won't be more than a couple of minutes. Please, go downstairs and wander round. Make yourself at home.'

'Really?'

'Really,' he smiles. 'I'll join you in a jiffy.'

The stairs are steep and I have to mind my head going

47

down. A long corridor, also book-lined, runs the length of the boat ahead of me, and a row of portholes are dotted at regular intervals high up along its right-hand side. They are too high to see out of. On the left at the bottom of the stairs is a small room that has the subdued look of a spare bedroom, its double bed covered by a dark blue cotton bedspread, with books covering one wall and a free-standing mirror leaning against another. The room is dark, lit by just four high portholes, facing east. There are some cardboard boxes piled in one corner of the room, a newish-looking folding bicycle leaning against them.

In the next room along, tiled in large white squares, is a generous-sized shower behind a large sheet of glass. I notice a pair of grey sweatpants draped over a chrome towel rail, and the smell of coal tar soap.

At the end of the corridor, its bleached floorboards covered with a Persian runner that is fraying at the edges, I pause – a doubtful intruder – before entering Angus's bedroom. Its size surprises me. It stretches across the boat's entire width, with portholes along both sides. Through the ones to the east I can see the dark bulk of a hull, of the boat next door. The light through the ones to the west is unimpeded and even though clouds are gathering and it is just beginning to rain, they admit the last of the diluted afternoon sun. A weak splash of wintry light swims fleetingly across the bed as I enter the room, briefly illuminating one half of the bedspread, which is rich and heavy, a patchwork tapestry of cottons and silks in indigo, emerald and gold.

Above the bed is an abstract oil painting of a horse's head, neck and back. The horse's head is thrown back, its mane awry and its nostrils flared. I lean closer to the painting, scrutinize the brushstrokes. It is interestingly turbulent but a bit too fussy. I don't like it.

On a low table beside the bed is a small pile of books. I cast my eye down their spines: a biography of Ella Fitzgerald; a Danish thriller; a recently published account of the Second World War. I notice that Angus sleeps on the same side of the bed as I do, or so I assume from the book pile. I scan the top of a large mahogany chest of drawers – Victorian, by the looks of it – for framed photographs. There are none.

In the bathroom that leads off Angus's bedroom there is a sizeable oval bath, sleek and modern, white, with one elegant, chrome mixer tap placed centrally. The wall behind the bath is mirrored, which gives an effective impression of depth in what is otherwise quite a narrow room. On the floor, a pair of hand-weights rests beside a copy of *Private Eye*. A navy-blue towelling bathrobe hangs on the back of the door. The aftershave I failed to recognize at the concert is on a shelf to one side of the basin. I peer closely at the label.

'How do you like it?'

Angus is in the doorway. He makes me jump.

'Your aftershave?'

He laughs.

'No. My pad.'

'I think it's a fantastic pad.'

'Oh, thank you. I'm genuinely pleased.'

'I do quite like your aftershave, too.'

'Do you now?' says Angus, one eyebrow raised. 'Well, that's very good to know.'

Upstairs, we contemplate the piano.

'Play me something.'

'What would you like?'

'Anything. Not jazz.'

'You don't like jazz?'

'No.'

'My darling girl, you haven't lived!'

He sits. He raises his hands above the keyboard, pauses, then releases them; they descend upon the keys like two birds coming to ground. He plays the opening of Bach's *Goldberg Variations*. Oh, I should have known he'd pull a stunt like that. Who wouldn't, if they could? Who would resist co-opting a virtuoso to invoke such easy surrender in the listener, with those opening notes, that cadence that rolls smoothly, effortlessly downhill and into the distance? And who would not be taken captive? I listen to Angus play and everything around me – the pictures, books and rain-streaked views outside – begins to blur;

and as if I am pulling away from my life, disconnected from everything but the potency of the music, I sense myself separating. A dizziness I remember from child-hood overcomes me, the kind I recall from banging my head too hard during a rough-and-tumble game, a soaring light-headedness that disembodies you tempor-arily before the pain kicks in. I feel removed, as if in some way I do not apply.

Confused, I seek bearings. I glance out of the window to the river beyond but because the view is foreign the sensation of abstraction intensifies and for a few seconds, maybe more, I do not understand where I am. This moment – its peculiar fullness – seems to belong in another phase. My thoughts expand and contract and reduce finally to the plainest longing: I want to put my head in Angus's lap. I want his fingers in my hair. I whisper something unsayable to him, under my breath. He will not hear it.

Outside, a sudden volley of raindrops beats against the windows.

Angus has stopped playing. He is staring down at the keys, as if mildly surprised by what he discovered there.

'That was beautiful.'

He turns sideways on the piano stool and looks up at me.

'Bach,' he replies, with a contented sigh. 'A great jazz musician.'

'So some people say.'

'They do indeed. You told me you play.'

'Yes, but nothing like you, obviously. You're a professional musician.'

'Play me something, Lucy.'

'You must be kidding.'

'Go on.'

'No way. I'm honestly no good.'

'For me? Just something?'

'No,' I repeat.

Especially not for you.

He rises from the piano stool.

'Tell me, Lucy,' he asks, 'do you always say no?'

His tone, quite suddenly, is assertive, and now the troubling, heady strangeness of the situation threatens to engulf me. In over my head I am, and how fast – how alarmingly fast – I am being swept along on this stretch of wide, grey water. I try to summon up my children, like a talisman, to keep me safe from where I am this minute, to detain me, prevent me from being carried away by a man in a boat. I picture my daughters, hair round their shoulders, glued to cartoons, oblivious to everything around them, including their mother. But the image has no imaginative force. Everything about it is situated elsewhere, so far away that it may as well not exist.

'No,' I reply, and Angus, correctly interpreting my sly, single-syllabled equivocation as the invitation that it is, takes a couple of steps towards me; and as he carefully inserts himself into my vision so that I can see nothing but him my memories of previous first encounters – thrilling discomposures long since safely archived – threaten suddenly to re-tell themselves in the present. Now, I understand all too clearly where I am. I am on the boundary of probity and licentiousness where good sense may prevail but folly and desire may, too. My weaknesses are declaring themselves but until either discretion or intemperance proves stronger I will remain at a border crossing, with no patrol here but myself. This is the last safe point. Beyond it, things will happen.

I realize the seriousness of this. I remember only too well what it is like never to have felt this way before; I am perfectly acquainted with that exquisite half-truth. Yet I never expected to encounter such complications again: I'm married; I thought I was safe. Compelled and stalled in equal measure by the promises and apprehensions of possibility, I hold back. I cannot endorse what I want to do, for my husband is real and I love him, so when it happens, when Angus lowers his head to kiss me on the lips, I turn my face away and stand, transported, as he kisses my hair instead – and then my neck, and after that my throat, and lower still, the V of skin unconcealed by my open-necked shirt. I close my eyes. I tell myself this is the most I can accept in the circumstances, convinced that I will need and want no more; that this will be sufficient for my future recollections of what might have happened but did not, this afternoon on the river. And while Angus's lips brush my left ear, my hands find their way to his hips – but not to the small of his back or around his neck, in which my face is now buried, so I can assure myself that I am no real part of this. And as his breath warms my head and he kneads the back of my neck as tenderly as I once caressed my babies' plump thighs, I believe I even congratulate myself for my self-control.

He releases me and looks down into my upturned face. Conspicuously, he is happy. I am shaking. I take a slight, faltering step backwards and we stand quietly, inches apart. He raises his right hand and with the back of it softly strokes my right cheek.

Don't take your hand away.

He takes his hand away.

I look out of the large window. The rain is easing.

'Ah, look,' says Angus, following my gaze. 'There's a break in the clouds. Come with me to the kitchen and I'll make us some tea. We can enjoy the light better in there.'

I will tell Mark. I will explain to him what has happened. I will tell my husband I didn't kiss Angus and if he asks me if I wanted to I will answer him honestly. I will tell him everything I am feeling at this moment because we promised each other we would never lie and if there is one promise I know I can keep, it is that; and because he knows me he will understand.

'I didn't kiss him.'

    'I don't need to know.'

    'But I didn't, I swear.'

    'Then spare me the details.'

    'There aren't any.'

    'Fine.'

    My head swims. I recall the dizziness I felt on the boat. I think, *Is this really now?*

    I ask, 'Is that all you can say?'

    'What do you want me to say?'

    I don't know. What I do know is that I want suddenly to have a knock-down, drag-out row with Mark in which I can accuse him of being cold and unreachable, though I am clearly in the wrong and should instead be grateful that I have a husband so strongly disinclined to outright opposition – even in this painful instance – that he will resort to silence rather than stoop to a raised voice. There is no situation in which Mark does not enjoy pursuing logic to its logical conclusion and if pressed, he can be derisive, even caustic, but he is more wont to adopt an attitude of lofty dispensation than antagonism. This often makes people feel patronized, which troubles him not in the least: he has a reason for repudiating conflict and it is sound.

That he wishes now to suspend discussion of marital transgression should not surprise me: I've often thought that if Mark could erase all evidence of vulnerability from himself he would, so that others wishing to know or care for him would encounter stamina and resourcefulness in place of a range of identifiable susceptibilities. I've sometimes wondered – aside from desire and fascination – what fundamental thing attracted me to him. Why did I marry a man who so strongly rejects help of any kind? Was it because I wanted to help him or because I knew I would never have to?

Yet today, when I might respectfully accept Mark's wish for quiet and even use it to my advantage (so I may creep away privately to assess my own shortcomings), all I want is a fight. I need something ruthless to happen. He seems so unjustifiably composed that I want to rough him up with my guilt and resentment; I want to scream, 'This is how you always win! This is how you always get what you want! You turn away and you will never hear me out. Damn you. Just damn you.'

Instead, I put my hand on my husband's arm to get his attention and when at last he looks me in the eye I say, 'Nothing happened, I promise.'

'Please,' he says. 'I'm busy. Just leave it.'

* * *

For days after Angus, I lay siege to the notion of love at first sight. Stupid. Illogical. Fanciful. And yet because I cannot explain myself to myself, slowly I give up, I give in. I don't know what is happening to me, except that something has already started to demolish what I can only think of as some internal rule of law, some code I had never thought to question. And whilst this sense of being dismantled is gradual, it is definitive also: my certitude, my faith in my own judgement, is utterly awry. This is what it's like to lose your reason. This must be what is meant by madness.

And yet, the truth is this: the very first time I saw Angus I thought to myself, *This is a man I could love,* and nothing could have felt more sane. I don't know why. The systemic conviction, the capsizing of previous certainties, is something I will never be able to explain, either to myself or anyone else. It wasn't even like a normal thought when it happened, it was more of a sensation – a voltaic jolt of inevitability and recognition combined. The lightning strike. Bang through every part of me. I guess that's precisely why people talk about lightning strikes, why they seem appropriate for moments like this. Piercing, scorching and electrifying, and once experienced, irreversible.

The confusion is mind-blowing.

Family life continues. The children go to school. Clothes are washed and meals produced but I no longer feel the ground beneath my feet. I float through the hours in a state of incomprehension, all ordinary plans supplanted by thoughts of Angus. I am surprised when it is time to go to bed and yet another day has passed.

Mark goes to London to visit his agent and a gallery owner; he is planning a retrospective next winter. On the days when I am out at work he warms up the shepherd's pies and chicken casseroles I have cooked for the girls. In between-times we talk almost non-stop, as if by doing so we will reimagine a narrative strong enough to overcome our disturbance and disorientation. All I want to talk about is Angus. I don't, of course. It would be indecent.

Oddly, we laugh quite a lot, much more than you might expect a couple to do when one person is in danger of falling overboard and the other is understandably stunned. Why is this? Our humour has admittedly assumed a darker complexion – sometimes it feels like a kind of demented release – but perhaps this is not as weird as it seems. I have no idea. Who knows how anyone else negotiates stuff like this?

We still niggle at one another. Occasionally, we raise our voices but we stop short of fighting. I think we are too terrified to do that. Instead, we reiterate everything that binds us and consider it evidence of fresh insight. We zoom in on our capacity to enjoy one another's company, run two jobs, and raise children together. Putting out the rubbish in the early-morning damp we remind ourselves of the fundaments of teamwork. While I lie in the bath and Mark brushes his teeth we agree that family matters most, yet in bed we are quiet, deflated.

'We're still us,' Mark whispers, his arms around my waist.

But doubt is there. It has interposed itself into the present.

Night-times, I lie awake. Beneath a plain, white-covered duvet, Angus's emerald-and-gold bedspread occupies me.

Mark props himself up on one elbow. He pulls the duvet down a little, strokes my shoulder. I freeze.

'Hey,' he says. 'I just want to be close to you.'

'You are close to me. We're close to each other.'

'You're close to the girls, Luce.'

I think of them, fast asleep, in rooms either side of ours. Most nights we look at them sleeping and marvel at the love they arouse. When Mark sleeps, it is very easy to love him, too: recumbent, he is within my grasp, unguarded and vulnerable. Sometimes at night, I reach out and stroke his hair.

I pull the duvet back up.

'I'm cold.'

Mark rests the back of his hand on my face.

'You are.'

He says we should have more sex.

'What?'

'Isn't the average married couple at it at least twice a week?'

'I doubt it.'

'How do you know?'

I don't, is the answer, and I am scared that it may be true; that beyond the four walls of our home, everyone else is at it hammer and tongs whilst we sleep fitfully beside each other, tense and vacillating. Mark's amatory decree has brought to the fore a hollowness that has been troubling me, and made more conspicuous a lassitude I have been trying hard to ignore. Yet with it comes a sense of relief that runs counter to this soul-sapping indifference, a sudden surge of pride in my husband for being a man who never beats about the bush. I am grateful. Mark has spared us both a drawn-out confession. He could have done otherwise.

'Do you think we could be bored?' I ask.

'What, us?'

'Yes.'

'Don't be silly.'

I think Mark thinks we're above boredom, and perhaps I do, too. And I am wondering whether it is the lie we have assumed as a truth – that we are somehow immune to ennui; that shared projects and busy lives may protect us from everything, including wearied physical appetites. Dullness and apathy is not our currency, Mark's and mine, at least not as far as we're concerned: we deal in vivid colour and joint enterprise; it's what we do, the way we define ourselves. It is how, as one, we evade the grey areas. So, we don't talk about the things that are wrong with us. I think we honestly believe there isn't anything. *Hubris* doesn't even begin to cover it.

In the meantime, emails fly back and forth.

'*You just come again,*' Angus writes, '*as soon as you are able. I'm here. I'm not going anywhere.*'

I say, 'Angus has asked me for supper.'

Mark shrugs.

I seek permission.

Mark says, 'Not mine to give.'

I suspect he believes we are bulletproof.

* * *

Angus is wearing his Nordic-style cardigan again, and a pair of navy cords.

'Cords,' my best friend Di used to say. 'Don't get me started on cords. Or cardigans. Kiss of death.'

When I was twenty-one, I had a date with a divorced forty-something man in tomato-red corduroys and it is something Di has chosen not to forget. He turned up at our flat with his wavy, blonde hair parted so strictly to one side that he looked like an exile from a BBC drama set in the forties and immediately I was overcome with such strong distaste that the thought of a whole evening with him filled me with panic. He wasn't wearing a cardigan, which might have added further period integrity to his look: he was sporting a navy-blue blazer, with anchors embossed on its brass buttons.

Di smiled apologetically at him as she tugged me forcibly by one arm into the kitchen.

'Are you serious?' she hissed. 'He looks like a Tory MP!'

'Well, he isn't.'

'What does he do?'

'Not a hundred per cent sure.'

'Don't give me that.'

I admitted that he insured ships for the UAE government from a glass-walled office in Blackfriars.

'Holy Mary, Mother of God! That's almost worse! Where did you find him?'

'A party.' I pulled away from her. 'And what's with the Catholic invocation? You're an atheist.'

'Religious people swear better. Were they all ancient at this party or were there other options?'

'I like ancient. They usually have something to say for themselves.'

'But he's not even your type.'

'He's interesting to talk to. Look, I'm not planning on sleeping with him.'

'What's the point, then?'

'I don't know. Maybe I just want a date.'

'Well, Jesus, who doesn't? But keep it simple! Pull a bloke in a club like the rest of us and be done with a simple once-over, why don't you?'

'I hate clubs. I hate once-overs. You know that.'

'You're a freak.'

I wonder what Di would think of me now, leaning against Angus's kitchen cupboard and watching him slice an onion into tiny pieces and with a long-bladed knife sweep its luminous splinters into a casserole dish of sizzling butter. He chops potatoes, carrots and red peppers into chunks and adds them to the gently frying onions, along with some diced pork, fresh sage and stock; then he sloshes in some white wine, stirs the whole lot, places a lid on the casserole dish and turns the gas down low. There is a pleasing rhythm and ease to his movements. I believe it may be contentment.

'Hello?' he murmurs. 'What are you smiling about?'

In some partially unfolded greaseproof paper on the worktop is a slab of brie, discharging itself around the edges. An unopened packet of Bath Oliver biscuits stands alongside. Angus, it seems, is planning an extended evening.

'Nothing much.'

'Really? Well, you look very cheerful, that's for sure.' He opens the fridge door, pulls out a bottle of white wine, raises it: 'Yes?'

At the table, we toast one another. Between us, there are fresh lilies, white. *Ah yes,* I think, *perfect confessional flowers.*

'What's this wood?' I tap the table. 'Is it elm?'

'It is! I'm impressed! Beautiful grain, don't you think?'

I trace the swirls of the grain, elongated like isobars, and wide apart. High pressure. A warm front.

'Lovely. You know that elm was used to make ships' keels because it bent well and didn't split?'

'I do, actually.'

'Right, but the strange thing is, it's only resistant to water if it's submerged. If you put elm wood on to wet ground it rots.'

'Really? Now, that I did not know.'

'It also doesn't burn very well; it spits a lot. You don't want it on an open fire.'

Angus grins and shakes his head, as if he has just heard a good joke.

'You really are a very surprising woman,' he says. 'You and your wood.'

'Not really,' I reply. 'And anyway, these days I only chop the stuff up occasionally. It's a very long time since I went up a tree, except for the fun of climbing it.'

'That in itself still sets you apart somewhat.'

'Who from?'

'Every woman I can think of.'

'Perhaps you need to think differently, or meet more women.'

'I don't think so. I like the one sitting right here. The first-ever tree surgeon to do so.'

On a crash course, it can take as little as eight weeks to become a tree surgeon but I took four months because I had two other part-time jobs at the time and not much spare cash. It seemed easier on both my bank account and my body, to take a little time; it spread the pain, in both senses. I was twenty-two, and for nearly a year I worked as an assistant cutter for the Forestry Commission in north Wales, where the scenery proved so enticing that I found myself armed with my camera almost as often as my chainsaw, and eventually, my growing interest in photography overrode my childish desire to prove that I could cut it in a job that really irritated my parents.

Photography was my first attempt at doing something I genuinely enjoyed. I felt capable when armed with a camera and comfortable with the conflicting senses of immersion and detachment that it produced. When I met Mark, I was on a one-year foundation course at Oxford Poly, and soon afterwards I began to take wedding pictures for friends, specializing in images of the things people generally don't see before the event, like a marquee refusing to stay up in a high wind and the caterers in extremis, or guests having a fag, or a disagreement, or a change of clothes in the car park. There was nothing special about them – these days such images are commonplace – but back then, they were popular.

For a while, I dreamed of being a good landscape photographer and thought maybe I could part-fund my travels that way but it was a tough market stuffed with talented and established people, and though a couple of agencies were happy to put some of my images into stock no one wanted to pay me much. I can see why. Although my early landscape photographs were tonally well-balanced and quite pretty they lacked theme and punch. In short, they were not really pictures you would look at twice. So, I learned to take photographs that gave the viewer somewhere more interesting to go. I came to understand the importance of the unexpected and no longer sought composure but disquiet. In amongst my favourite images a pack of skittering cats interrupts the passage of a wedding party in Udaipur; and in a panoramic shot of the Wadi Qelt desert in Israel, a nomadic woman is just visible bottom left, running into the frame, alone – her movement and sense of dispatch both affecting and faintly unreal in such a vast, lunar-like space.

Later still, with Mark's unforgiving eye on mine, I found myself on the lookout for quirks that previously had intimidated me. Geometric shadows and the blunt shock of dark abutting light at an acute angle grew as alluring to me as a honey-lit human face or a near-flawless vista messed up around one edge. I experimented for a while with the surprise of shapes and I surprised myself. In my first picture to win an award, a wild pig is snuffling through a rubbish pile in Giza while a boy looks on impassively; the Sphinx is clearly visible in the top right-hand corner of the photograph. The point is not the juxtaposition of filthy swine with iconic monument: the pig with its foraging snout has exhumed a cardboard box bearing the word *Pepsi* along one side, the boy is drinking a bottle of Pepsi, and a billboard advertising Pepsi is visible in the background, in soft focus. Each flourish of red script moves in imperfect diagonal steps across the image. The picture is called *America*.

'What about now?' Angus asks. 'Is it only portraits?'

'Yes, mainly. I still like landscapes but we don't really travel together now, Mark and I. Not since the kids were born. He goes alone.'

'That sounds a bit lonely.'

'He loves it.'

'No, for you, I mean.'

'I'm okay. The twins keep me occupied.'

'I'm sure they do. Shame about the tree surgery, though. Sounds funky.'

For pudding, Angus has made crème brûlée.

'You're a wonderful cook, Angus.'

'Years of living alone, sweetheart.'

'How alone?'

'Very alone.'

'You've never married?'

'No.'

'But surely you've lived with people.'

'Never.'

I don't know what I had expected but it is not this. Already, I have thought about it a lot: how Angus might have lived, and with whom; how long for, and how meaningfully.

'Not even once?'

'No. I mean, some toing and froing between their places and mine, but that's it.'

A man of sixty who has never lived with anyone is someone with likely, even serious, defects. And yet, I am flooded with a sensation I recognize from long ago. It is not a sensation I expected to feel again and it's a sensation I would do well to ignore – that any woman in a situation

68

like this would do well to ignore – for jostling with shock
and common sense are wild and inappropriate thoughts:
*I would not stand for that from you. I could be the one. I know
how.*

'Thought about it once or twice,' he adds. 'Thought
better of it.'

I look at Angus and I feel the difference between us.
What could be better than living with another person?
What nicer than waking beside them, so that you may
never feel alone? Except that you may still feel alone, and
neither marriage nor partnership can entirely prevent
that. Maybe Angus accepts this more readily than most
and lives his life accordingly. Or maybe he is selfish, or
lazy, and when commitment is required of him he finds
reasons for sidestepping the necessary effort and resolve.
This is all conjecture, of course; I hardly know the man.
Still, I would place a substantial bet on his thinking
marriage essentially dishonest.

'Have you never wanted to live alone, Lucy?'

'No. I love being married.'

'Well, you have a lovely husband, of course.'

Angus's elbows are on the table, his hands clasped
before him in an attitude of expectation, and quite
suddenly, I am outraged. If this man is asking to hear
exactly what my husband means to me, then let him hear
it, smooth bastard. He is too convinced of himself: worse,
he is too convinced of me.

So, I tell him a tale of the four walls around me and my husband and how we keep them upright. I tell him how Mark never fails to surprise me. I describe what we have built together. I am merciless: I say things like, 'Not that you will understand, not having been married.' I explain that an elderly friend advised us the week before our wedding that in marriage there is no stopping place and that no one ever tells you that – and I recount how often we say to one another that our friend was absolutely right and while it's a real bugger at times having nowhere to pull over, there is no one in the world with whom either of us would rather keep going.

Angus has been listening intently. Now, he is leaning back in his chair. His arms are folded across his chest, fingers tucked into his armpits. He says, 'That's a formidable partnership, by the sounds of it.'

'Nothing comes close.'

'But you're here with me.'

'Yes, I am.'

One of the flowers is drooping slightly over the side of the vase. I touch it, lightly.

'Lucy.'

'Yes.'

'Look, I don't make a habit of seeing married women, I can promise you, so I'm going to ask you something.'

'Go ahead.'

'What is this?'

Fish away, I think, *you on your boat.*

'Because – and I'll be honest, sweetheart – I think I'm in some serious trouble here.'

'Isn't it usually the case,' I say, 'that in situations like this, it is more about oneself than the other person?'

Angus flinches. Outside, on the water, a police launch speeds past close by, its lights on full. Its wash, by the time it reaches *Verity*'s curved frame, has almost played out. It makes no impact.

'If it is the case,' Angus says, 'should I be wary?'

'No. We should be realistic.'

He nods.

'We probably should.'

We. We are already talking *we.*

He drives me to the station.

At the first set of traffic lights, he asks, 'May I call you?'

I shake my head.

'Texts?'

'Yes. Or email. But no calls. I explained that already.'

'You did. Sorry.'

I stare at the traffic lights, willing them to stay red. When Mark is driving and we are talking, it's generally my only chance to chip in during a conversation.

Angus says, 'I tell myself whenever I'm with you, and

71

quite often when I'm not, "Angus, no!" I tell myself not to think about you. I try very hard not to think about you.' The lights change and he pulls away. 'But it doesn't work. You're there all the same, all the time.'

I listen to the muffled rub of his clothes as he changes gear.

He says, 'Is it okay with you if I pull over just ahead?'

I nod.

He manoeuvres on to double yellow lines, briefly switching the hazard lights on and then off again, and kills the ignition. The engine's purr succumbs and for a moment neither of us moves. The sudden quiet is jarring: my ears are ringing slightly and I can hear Angus breathing. We twist in our seats to face each other and in the car's muted hush the rustle of fabric and leather seats is so obtrusive that suddenly I am fraught with self-consciousness. Angus releases his seat belt, which retracts abruptly. Cars are streaking past outside, I'm at risk of being late for my train, and he is reaching across my lap and taking my hands in both of his, and squeezing them, firmly. My engagement ring digs sharply into the flesh of his thumb: whether it hurts him, he does not indicate. He is holding my hands in the manner of someone about to deliver serious news.

He asks me, very politely, 'Is it okay with you if I kiss you?'

I nod, again.

* * *

Mark says, 'This puts a rather different spin on things.'

'Is that all you can say?'

'It happens.'

'Not to us!'

'Well, clearly it has.'

'I feel awful.'

'I can understand that.'

'I won't see him again.'

'That's your call.'

'It's our call! I won't see him if you ask me not to.'

'It's nothing to do with me. Let's get that straight.'

'How can you say that? I'm your wife!'

'Luce,' Mark's tone is unequivocal. 'I'm going over to the barn. I've got work to do. So have you.'

'Can't you at least tell me what you think?'

'I think you must do what you need to do.'

'Don't you care?'

There is a pause before he says, 'I'm not even going to answer that.'

My phone screen lights up with Angus's name.

Mark makes a face as if to say, 'Oh yeah?'

'You'll see him again,' he says. 'It's a given. I'm off.'

'Mark, please don't go. Talk to me properly, I beseech you!'

'You beseech me?' he says, turning away. 'What are you, the Book of Common Prayer?'

I sit down, heavily, as if it were the end of the day and

not the beginning. There's a bran flake I must have missed when wiping the table after breakfast. I rub it to dust between my fingers until just one resolute, sharp nugget remains. I read Angus's text. *'How are things your end, my angel? Let me know. Xxx'*

Time passes.

It's so dark in this kitchen. *Bloody winter.* But it's not just the winter. Until Mark comes in and switches on every last overhead halogen bulb, it's always dark in this house. The best light is in the barn, where Mark is.

Angus texts again. *'Sweetheart, do you like* La Traviata? *I can get tickets. Xxx'*

'Yes,' I reply. *'Tell me when! Xxx'*

Five weeks.

This is all it takes.

This is how long it is until Angus says he loves me.

'What, are you sure?'

'More sure than I've ever been in my life.'

'Oh, Angus.'

He gathers me up in his arms and rolls me over and then he says it again because now that the unsaid has been said – and the not-done been done – he wants to hear what it sounds like. He tells me he has been trying not to say it, or think it, and has been doing everything he can to put it out of his mind but now he wants to declare himself over and over, on that same, sweet, reverent afternoon.

'I love you,' he says, 'I love you, I love you, I love you.' He strokes my hair; his eyes are shining. 'Have you seen *The Life of Brian*?'

He is heavy on top of me. Laughing hurts.

'Yes. Why?'

It's because, Angus explains, he feels like the hermit whose twenty-year vow of silence is broken when Brian jumps into his dusty hollow wanting somewhere quiet to hide, but instead, the hermit is animated into a frenzy of loud declarations.

'You daft man.'

'But I'm him!' says Angus. 'I want to jump up and down. I want to shout it from the rooftops: "I love Lucy Burdett!"'

Five weeks, four encounters. I didn't think love happened that way.

'It never has, with me,' says Angus, adamantly. 'This is a first.'

'Yes, well, you say that—'

Tenderly, he places his fingers over my mouth. The low light from the window is playing upon his eyelashes, which are damp. I feel the sting of tears in my own eyes.

'Shhh, my angel. I say it, Lucy, because it's true.'

And so, in the early hours of the evening, when we

have dozed a while and woken again to the fresh joy of one another, I say it back. I tell him I love him too, not because it is true but because I feel that such a gift deserves not just any old thank-you. It is true, though. I do love him, perhaps even as much as he says he loves me. I just hadn't planned on letting myself think that way and had I been him I would have held out longer. Just to be sure.

Back home, at 2 a.m., I steal into the bed containing my husband. He does not wake. I do not sleep.

There is no innocence left. I am on constant alert. When my phone pings, I jump as if stung. I anticipate reprimand, imagine when collecting my children from school the outrage of other, better, parents, who do not know that a deserter is in their midst. From Mark, I expect rows and recriminations but he is unspeaking; pale and constrained.

Most days now, I linger, when I take hot drinks to the barn. I say things like, 'I love watching you paint, it reminds me of when we first met.' The words sound flimsy and ostentatious. I feel numb.

I don't know what I am hoping for. I think perhaps I want my husband to feel visible, and that all is not lost. I watch as he reaches for a small brush, licks his right thumb and forefinger, presses the hairs of the brush together and twists them into a sharp point.

The cold tap over the sink drips insistently: it's been doing so for weeks. It doesn't impinge on Mark but for me, in the difficult, inhibited silence, it is as if our awkwardness is being counted out in half-seconds; the drip, drip, drip of marital erosion, falling daily on deaf ears. I twist around and tighten the tap.

'Mark? Do you not want to say something?'

From a pile of compressed metal tubes on the table, Mark selects one, unscrews its lid and squeezes a snail-shaped slick of navy blue on to a smooth, plastic board that is already daubed with pale, skin-coloured smudges. With the small brush, he introduces tiny dabs of blue to a couple of them. Contemplating the canvas where – as an eighteenth-birthday gift commissioned by her wealthy father – a teenage girl is coming of age in tender shades of fresh complexion, he says, 'Yes. It needs a new washer. I'll fix it.'

I am adrift. Remorse and pain are like distant islands across a stretch of grey water – outlines only, remote but in sight. Even more alarming than feeling everything at once, with Angus, is feeling almost nothing now, here with Mark. Perhaps during our nights together, like a succubus Angus drains me dry – and I return home a husk, desiccated and empty.

'I honestly didn't mean it to go this far.'

77

'No one ever does.'

But they do. They mean it to go this far because it's what they want. They mean to put obstacles in their own way. They mean to block their best route home. They mean it. I mean it. Why?

Mark moves closer to the painting. He studies the girl's brow, his expression steady but perplexed. Then he steps back, rubs his left arm across his forehead. He reminds me that he has four commissions to finish by Easter, he is teaching over the holidays and there's Cornwall coming up this summer.

He says, 'Luce, I don't have anything spare right now, for this.'

'I don't love him like I love you.'

He blinks hard.

'Love him?'

Simultaneously, we try to register the impact of the blow I have inflicted.

'Mark, it's different. It's nothing like us.'

'Love him?' he repeats.

The shock is not yet absorbed but the damage is done. I think, *Now, we can never go back to the way things were.*

'I had no idea that's where you were going with this.'

'Neither did I.'

I move closer to my husband and raise my hand to touch his face, but he says, 'No. I'll see you later,' and I

know better than to persevere. He turns away. He will not
hear me now.

Feverishly, we burn away the small hours.
    'Country girl, are you still awake? Xxx'
    'For you, yes, yes and yes. Xxx'
    'How soon can you come up again? Xxx'
    'Saturday. Xxx'
    'Do you fancy the cinema? Xxx'
    There is so much to know, so much to learn, so much
to offer. We draw maps of ourselves, trace around our
likes and dislikes, give shape to our strengths and dreams
– to our weaknesses as well, though we make those sound
like bewitching peculiarities, charming quirks that the
other person (and only the other person) might especially
appreciate. Back and forth and back and forth we go, our
emails fleet, smooth, silent. He sometimes asks if we can
speak instead but I won't talk to Angus on the phone. I
made it crystal clear, that first afternoon in *Verity*'s hold.
    'Isn't that a bit absurd?' he asks.
    He doesn't understand why it matters so much but I
can't speak directly to Mark on the phone and I want so
badly to be even-handed.
    'Parity is surely beside the point in this instance, *ma
cherie*,' Angus persists.

'Exactly,' I reply.

'I don't understand.'

I tell him I will never give him the one thing Mark will never have.

'Do you see any irony in that?'

'I am choosing not to.'

My husband is profoundly deaf. It isn't the first thing people notice about him. On the contrary, Mark manages his lack of hearing so well that people are usually astonished, even awed, when it dawns on them he hasn't heard a word they've said. A lot of them don't realize it at all, although when the subject comes up, which invariably it does sooner or later, occasionally someone will say, 'I did wonder if there was something.' However, because Mark's speech and his skill for lip-reading are both damn near perfect, it doesn't happen often – and those people who wonder can never quite define what that something is, either.

Women especially are enthralled. 'He's amazing!' they exclaim. 'Just incredible!' They look from him to me, and then back to him again: they tell me how dynamic he is, how clever, how good with our children. If they tell me how gorgeous he is, too, then I know what they are really thinking because people are very transparent; it doesn't occur to most of them until they experience it first hand, that a man or woman's sex appeal is entirely unrelated to the range or frequency of their hearing. You don't have to have a deaf husband for long before you come to recognize others' poorly concealed astonishment that this, in fact, is the case.

No one would think to use the word 'disabled' about Mark but he was incarcerated from babyhood in a remote, dull buzz that regressed to absolute silence by the time he was ten, or thereabouts. Without his hearing aids, a fanfare of trumpets in the same room would not register, and even with his aids, it would make almost no impact. He has never heard himself breathe. Born, however, with the ability to make out a few very faint sounds in the lower register he had just enough hearing as a small child to get by with a minimum aural grasp of some deep tonal shifts. These muted grunts and rumbles helped him to learn a bit about weight and emphasis in speech but nothing more: he has never heard a proper word in his life and even if by some miracle he could suddenly hear, he wouldn't recognize one, either. However, until he was eight or nine he managed okay by keeping quiet and learning to lip-read more or less by default. After that, his peers took exception to the withdrawn child who didn't sound right; they mocked and taunted him and he began to suffer. His parents dug into their savings, and a speech therapist with a coronet of blonde hair took on the boy with the deformed vowels and transformed him.

It took years of hard work but Mark's vowels separated, his consonants sharpened and his voice softened. He practised long and hard, learned tricks to cover for himself when faced with an immobile upper lip, a strong foreign accent or a beard, all of which make lip-reading difficult to impossible. But his speech therapist could not alter the fact that Mark had never heard a light breeze through leaves, or water trickling from a tap: nor had his attention been caught by the clink of a spoon upon china or the whip of a quickly turned page, or a thousand other things. Like the letter S, for example. S is the highest sound on the vocal register; I hadn't known that before I met Mark. It is why, when he is dog-tired, his S's elide a little and the slurring of speech that is common to people with profound hearing loss is marginally evident in him. I tried to imagine, when we first got together, how it must have been to learn the feel of a sound you will never hear, to get it right against your palate, and to trust that you knew how. He couldn't explain it adequately, there being no common language to describe and discuss speech when one of you can't hear it. It took him several months to get it perfect, was his answer.

Ssssseveral. Sssseek. Sssssomething. Sssssuccinct.

'That was a bit of a bummer,' says Mark. 'Suck-Sinkt. Not the easiest word.'

82

Mark and I live in a couple of tiny farm cottages knocked into one, with a barn across the yard which the local planners won't let anyone convert into a home, so instead we adapted the barn into a studio for Mark, with a bathroom and a sofa-bed at one end for visitors who want a bit of beams-and-rafters romance but don't mind the discomfort. The house is small for four of us, and so low-ceilinged that Mark has to bend his head to get through its doorways, but the barn is why we bought the place. In its cavernous space, shared with a number of pipistrelle bats we are not at liberty to evacuate, Mark can spread out several large canvases at once. He keeps a set of drums in there, too, at some distance from his easels and frames, and sometimes in the evenings he wanders back over to the barn and beats the hell out of them. Judging by the look on his face when he's at it, anyone watching him drumming would be forgiven for thinking that he is intensely angry, but he isn't. He is simply abandoned. He used to look like that in bed, with me. He is at his least restrained when lost in a rhythm he can feel.

I reckon Mark is pretty musical, which is heart-breaking for he has never heard a note above the D below Middle C. He can still just about detect it now, but only with the help of the powerful hearing aids that give him access to a narrow band of bass sound, and when I ask him what it sounds like he produces a raspish *nuuurrrr* from the back of his throat, off-key. In fact, you'd think that music would be the one thing Mark might have given a miss but he longs for song, so much so that with prodigious determination he learned the ballads – or at least a fair smattering of them – that found their way, unimpeded, into the consciousness of his teenage friends. With the television volume turned up full and lyrics written on pieces of paper torn from school exercise books, Mark would sit in front of *Top of the Pops* straining not only for the faintest sound but for its variation, riveted by the body language of the singers that itself provided important additional clues about pitch and mood. Self-teaching has been an essential instrument of Mark's survival, so his commitment to memorizing tunes he would never hear himself was not the exercise in futility that some privately believed it to be. It was evidence of a childhood resolve not to be excluded from ordinary life more than he already was; not least from the sweet and easy pleasures of popular culture and the opportunities for camaraderie that it provided, that were so effortlessly enjoyed by his contemporaries.

Now, he has a repertoire that begins with early Abba and ends around the time that Queen were on the wane and Chris de Burgh well into his stride, and somewhere along the line the bass beat of the *Panorama* theme tune found its way in. This was a notable exception, as a solo human voice is easier to decipher than a mess of instruments, and songs sung by individuals were much easier for Mark to learn than anything performed by groups – which accounts for a final collection with heavy leanings towards Eric Clapton, Tina Turner, Rod Stewart, Lionel Richie and George Michael. Stalwarts admittedly, each of them, but deafness is not a prerequisite for broad musical taste.

Mark works hard to stay in tune. He sings daily, expecting me to correct him when he slips off-key, which is lots. 'Money, Money, Money' is a breakfast-time favourite. I object to it on the grounds that money is an unseemly everyday subject when children are present but Mark doesn't care. The truth is, I'm bored with it: we've been married sixteen years and that's a lot of 'Money, Money, Money'. 'Lady in Red' I get in bed quite often. 'I Am Sailing'. 'Wonderful Tonight'. Mark is by no means melodic and his higher register is grating but you would expect that and I'd be mad to object to a husband who wants to sing love songs to me. How many wives have that? 'Dancing Queen' he likes to dance to with the kids. If turned up loud enough anything with a strong, reverberative pulse that he can pick up through his feet will do but he has never known the perfect, aching beauty of Bach, Mozart or Handel: he will never experience the lavish grandeur of Beethoven, Schubert's easy turn of phrase or the impeccable frugality of Corelli. He has no more concept of plainsong, or the tremulous echo of the countertenor, than the ping of a microwave oven. With all his might, he once bent his mind around three or four Verdi arias but tragically late, when he could hear nothing of them.

When I met him, Mark's life had already swerved off a number of courses it might otherwise have taken. It has never gone in quite the direction he wanted it to and while you could say the same is true for many people, for Mark deafness put paid to a lot of dreams – like becoming a drummer in a rock band or joining the army, under whose protective umbrella he was raised. Mark is built like his father, David, who was a brigadier. He has the same strong, dense body, the same spry intellect and a near-identical tenacity and resilience. He tends naturally towards the stringent and enjoys the requirements of demanding activities and tricky terrain, whether actual or metaphorical. He is more animated by impediments than anyone I've ever known. But the military doesn't do a great line in deaf personnel. I don't think the army would have suited him anyway.

Painting does, however, requiring neither hearing nor extensive social intercourse. Mark likes best of all to paint landscapes, in oils mostly, though occasionally he switches to watercolours. He has painted quite a lot overseas, African skies and Greek seas for the London market, but the quixotic light and contrasts of the British land-scape move him most. Even so, while his landscapes account for eighty per cent of his work, what mainly pay the bills are not moody Celtic panoramas but traditional, individual portraits. Opulent and splendid but visually articulate as well – which is what I believe sets them apart – they are mostly commissioned by banks, law firms and wealthy private-sector businesses, although there are lots of individual commissions, too. Mark has three pictures in the National Portrait Gallery now: two are of well-known British film actresses; the other, a controversial former Cabinet Minister. This has not only raised Mark's profile but also tripled the value of his work.

Painting is something Mark originally did in his spare time because he loves it and has real talent. Why he never went to art school I still don't fully understand, and neither does his former art teacher, though he says it was because he never believed painting would make him a decent living. He was wrong. Mark's serendipitous encounter with an investment banker, when he was at Oxford reading History, changed everything. The bank-er's moderate-sized but prosperous firm was sponsoring a portrait prize through the university, so in between study-ing, swimming and sleeping with almost as many women as there were weeks in the year, Mark stretched a large canvas with some difficulty under the low eaves of his tiny college room and produced a huge, swaggering study of his best friend, Jay.

Jay is a large, amiable African-American. He and Mark met at a Hampshire boarding school that was densely populated by confident, Anglo-Saxon sons of British professionals and they hit it off immediately; a couple of oddballs in a straitjacket. Jay's father was an American film director of some note who travelled all over the world, his mother a film actress of Scottish descent who mainly stayed home in New York but had a thing about English public-school education. She liked the neo-Gothic architecture, said Jay, and all those sweeping lawns: they gave her a sense of history and space that she wished her son to appreciate and to aim for himself. She also felt strongly that Jay should be equipped with Latin and Greek. Jay's white parents plucked him out of a hostel in Harlem when he was six months old, or so the story goes. Jay has always wondered about his drugged-out, teenage mother. I have, too. He is a magnificent man and she is missing out on him – if she is even alive, still. He's a paediatrician now, in Truro.

That painting changed Mark's life. It features a glistening, vivacious Jay with a basketball under one arm and a viola partially balanced along the other. *Ready to Play* is its title, which is just the kind of appellation you come up with when you are twenty. The painting's background is all swathes of rich, scarlet velvet (a roll of which Mark found in a charity shop) and dark, mulch-green shadows. In the foreground, Jay is wearing tight running shorts that showcase his thighs to obvious advantage and a long, heavily brocaded jacket. It's a dog's breakfast of a portrait but it works really well. The baroque background is a piss-take but it gave Mark the chance to demonstrate his talent for painting cloth as well as skin.

Ready to Play won First Prize – three thousand quid, which was a lot of money in the mid-eighties – plus a commission to undertake a traditional portrait of the firm's outgoing chairman. Except that Mark's portrait wasn't traditional, in terms of ambience at least, because he managed to capture something essential and in this case distinctly discomfiting about the smooth-fleshed man inside the pinstripe. The picture so reeked of en-titlement that you could practically smell the musk of expensive, old-fashioned shaving soap and the delicate, muzzy scent of cashmere from which the suit was made, warmed by the chairman inside it who looked as if he was rarely anything other than exactly the right tempera-ture.

Mark invested the three thousand quid immediately. He put the money towards a deposit on a tiny, one-bedroomed flat on the outskirts of Oxford that he rented to a couple of medical students. The rest of the deposit he borrowed from his father, although in three years he had paid it back with earnings from word-of-mouth commissions. By then, the property market had boomed and the flat was worth a mint so Mark took out a second mortgage and bought another one. By the time I met him, at a party when he was thirty-five and I was twenty-six, he owned two flats, one of which produced just enough income to allow him to paint full-time and one of which – in central Oxford – he lived in by himself.

I remember what I was wearing at that party. A dark green roll-neck jersey, long black boots, and one of my favourite skirts, red wool, very short, A-line, with silver thread running in fine vertical stripes through the wool. My diamanté earrings had a slightly bauble-like appearance. It was August but the party was in someone's garden and it was unseasonably cold outside.

'Well, hello,' said Mark, smiling lazily. He was lolling against the trunk of a short cherry tree, wine glass in one hand. 'You look like Christmas.'

'Thanks.' I observed his checked shirt and Levi's. 'You don't.'

'Mmmm!' He shifted slightly and his smile changed; it held itself to account, somehow. 'What do I look like, then?'

Self-regarding, I thought.

'Self-regarding,' I said.

Two months after that party, Mark hid a shiny new set

of keys to his flat in my trainers. This was a man whose romantic commitments had previously run to not much more than sex followed by breakfast, followed by a steady flow of flirtatious one-line faxes until the next encounter. I wasted no time. I moved in, threw a few cushions of my own around the place, established a row of lipsticks on the bathroom shelves and upgraded Mark's mugs. I bought some nicer underwear, a set of gleaming white bath towels, and replied when Mark was out to the women who sent faxes asking whether he was in, with the words, *I'm afraid not but I'm Mark's girlfriend, Lucy. Can I give him a message for you?*

'This is it, isn't it,' said Mark, drily, a few months later. 'I think we'd better get married. What do you think?'

What I thought was, *Gosh, is that a proposal?*

Mark put down the tea towel he was holding – we were drying up after supper – and took both my hands in his.

'Luce,' he said, 'did you hear me? Will you marry me?'

'Oh, yes please.'

We kissed hurriedly; not like a couple with a whole lifetime ahead but as if one of us were boarding a train that was due to depart. I can even remember thinking, *Slow down, what's the rush?* but I had no answers. My ears were ringing slightly, as if I were dizzy. Mark looked down at me and said, 'I love you very much,' and I said, 'I love you, too,' and with our arms wrapped round each other we stood for a while, nuzzling, until Mark – noticing the tears in my eyes – pulled back, frowning, and asked, 'What's the matter?'

'Tell me it's real.'

'Of course it's real!' He laughed, and then he said softly, 'You'll be wanting a nice engagement ring.'

'I will!'

I left the ring behind once, on Angus's bedside table when we were first together; it's the only time in my life I have mislaid it, albeit briefly. I always take it off at night, and I remember thinking I mustn't forget it. I had to get Angus to turn the car around when we were already on our way to the station.

'Honestly, nutcase,' said Angus.

I thought, *Angus, you have no idea.*

Hot waves of anxiety rippled down my back as I let myself back in to retrieve my precious stones from the bedroom, which was now so quiet that I could hear the tick of the alarm clock. Sweating with relief, I put the ring back on.

That such a thing might happen. That I might be on a houseboat on the Thames in London at eight o'clock on a school morning, fishing around for my engagement ring many miles away from the children in Year Three (with whom I have volunteered to plant spring bulbs at eleven o'clock), while Angus who did not give me the ring and to whom therefore I did not properly belong, waited in a car on the Embankment. That such a thing happened astonishes me still. As an emblem of my own shame it remains pretty hard to beat but in fairness I wasn't altogether myself at the time. (I tell Angus often what a shock he was to me then – and is, even now: 'You're the shock of my life,' I say. 'Well, you're the love of mine,' he answers.)

When I reached school by ten-thirty that morning I was elated: on time, still intact and where I was supposed to be. *This is possible*, I told myself, *all things are possible.* The children seemed sweeter to me than usual. The sun was shining through the windows in the corridor outside the main classrooms, its rays intercepted by the plane trees in their path. Their branches and emerging leaves threw shivering lines across Millie, Callum, Josie, Oliver, Lauren and Liam, as they struggled excitably into their coats. The chosen few, ready to dig. I looked at these lovely children and wanted to hug them tightly but there's plenty in the rules about not doing that – and certainly not just because, intoxicated by ardour, you suddenly feel the whole world amended.

'What are you up to right now, my darling? xxx'
Bits of woodchip crack under my feet.

'*Stacking log-pile with Mark.*'

'*Can you visit next weekend?*'

'What does he want?' Mark asks. 'It is him, isn't it.'

'*. . . Because if you can, I want to kiss every inch of your beautiful body, very, very slowly. xxx*'

Mark sighs heavily.

'He's just asking me for a meal or something; if that's possible with you, of course.'

My husband looks at me pityingly. 'Do me a favour.'

I regard my mobile phone. It is as if it has a life of its own, now improbably connected with mine. A current of shame passes through me as I tap my assent on to the screen.

Mark throws a couple of logs to one side. For a while, we continue to stack in silence. Eventually, he says, '*Fait accompli.* What day are you going, and what exactly do you propose I do with the kids? The long-range forecast is lousy.'

I should care. I should pay attention to long-range forecasts. But my capacity to care is reduced and my attention span narrowed. My world has blown open in a blaze of colour and light and now my vision is so contracted by the glare that I am half-sighted, blundering.

My phone buzzes.

'*Fantastic! Are you happy to eat swordfish? xxx*'

Mark says, 'Jesus! Does this guy have nothing better to do than text my wife?'

* * *

Angus opens *Verity*'s front door. He is wearing his navy bathrobe. His hair, slicked back from his forehead, is glistening from a shower. He pulls me towards him, kicks the door shut, lifts my coat from my shoulders and lets it drop to the floor. 'Leave it,' he says, when I move to pick it up.

Taking my face in his hands, he bends to kiss me. His thumbs are in the hollows of my cheek. His fingers brush my ears, sweep the nape of my neck, knit into my hair. 'My darling you,' he murmurs. He is breathing fast. I untie his bathrobe, discover him inside it; I press my belly against his.

When we make love, I love to watch his face change. First, his expression is eager, hungry, then tender, longing, almost mystified. Later, losing himself, it is something bordering on the savage. The first time, it shocked me – his ferocity. He growls with pleasure, staring hard into my eyes, seeking me, not satisfied until I am staring back, stupefied once more and biting my lower lip so hard that it hurts afterwards: more than once, I draw my own blood. He is relentless, he pitches me this way and that, pins me down the way we both love, watching my face for the signs he has come to understand, listening to my voice, brushing my closed eyes with his mouth, and when I open them he is smiling down at me, saying, 'I love you I love you I love you I love you,' over and over, and he is so deft I can bear it no longer and I am over and over, too.

'Oh,' Angus moans, 'my angel,' and I, emergent, watch in wonder as everything about him that is contained is cast aside in favour of magnificent negligence. He cleaves to me, cries out, revealed and surrendered, and here in his arms, in his exquisite agony, I am restored. To initiate such tremors through that sturdy frame of his and to be unearthed so, myself: it is disclosure of the sweetest kind.

Coming to, he cradles my face with both his hands and kisses me deeply and slowly, and how I love it this way. I don't think there is a thing he can do that betters this.

'Oh, my darling.'

I pull him down to lie along the length of my body, aware of his weight.

'Lie on me,' I tell him.

'I'll crush you.'

'Don't be silly, you never do. Lie on me.'

He brushes a strand of my hair from my forehead, which he strokes, softly.

'You are very bossy.'

'I am.'

'Well, you want to watch it.'

'I do?'

'You do. Otherwise, I might have to take charge of you.'

'You just did.'

And he is very solid. Yet his skin is soft like a child's. I think it may be softer than the skin of any man I have known. I am intoxicated by the smell of him. I bury my face in his chest. I feel, at last, located.

'Nutcase,' he says, after a little while, 'you can't breathe.'

'Oh, but I can,' I say. 'See?'

Angus laughs. He says, 'I could never go back now, to life before you.'

Angus's parents were returning home from supper at the house of some friends, and it was a boy just two months older than Angus – intoxicated by a liberty that Angus was yet to experience – who caused the accident that killed them both before they reached it. They were very close to home, as it happened, on the notoriously sharp corner of a road that otherwise ran straight as a canal for a good quarter of a mile. Angus thinks his father tried to swerve to avoid the vehicle that bore down on them but no one is quite sure what happened except that the boy-driver just kept on coming and time was not on their side. The net effect was a head-on collision of such velocity and intensity that Angus's father's internal organs were pulverized, compressed by the steering wheel that rammed into his torso at a combined speed of ninety miles an hour. Angus's mother, who was not wearing a seat belt, exited the car through the wind-screen and most likely ricocheted from the roof of the other vehicle on to the road. Her head, caught as it had been on something (the police thought it was probably a slice of mutilated, inverted bonnet) became partially detached from her neck. All that detached from the seventeen-year-old survivor of the tragedy – if 'survivor' you could call the mute paraplegic he became – were his retinas. The force of the crash caused his optic nerves to sever and he was blinded at the moment of impact. People tried to spare Angus the facts of the matter at the time but without success: there were witnesses, police reports, an inquest.

When Angus first told me all this – over that tea together in the draughty cafe after the concert – I asked him how you survive something so appalling. I remember him reaching for a teaspoon on the table, turning it over and over, and saying, 'You get used to it, sweetheart, just like anything else.'

But it isn't just like anything else. When the accident destroyed his parents, Angus, like his mother, was arbitrarily tossed to one side of his own existence. Healing took place over the years. There was a kind godmother who provided a home that he could call his own for as long as he needed to; immersion in the study of music; college friends. He says these all helped. However, those around him at the time of the accident were so concerned with the immediate mopping-up of the mess that any lasting effects upon him were, perhaps understandably, barely considered. It might have seemed that the impact upon a seventeen-year-old boy of this sudden, family wipeout was most potent in its immediate aftermath, yet the greatest repercussions were chronic. Reconfigured by loss, Angus learned early on how to survive without others, and in this way, he was damaged for life. Some lessons, if learned too young, can't be integrated by a person. There are injuries no one can treat, that a boy on the verge of manhood cannot wholly sustain and live an easy life.

It is so visible to me in my lover, this invisible breakage, and it unsettles me. It is the thing to which I attribute some of Angus's quirks, like his willingness to consume food at any hour; like the fact that he regards laying a table as absurd. In fact, his aversion to the rites that bind others is so strong it's almost as if he believes they might somehow imperil his freedom. His mother must have laid tables, and his godmother too, when she stepped into the breach. When I do, he is amused. 'You're such a mum,' he says, as I neatly align our forks.

But it's other things, too. Christmas and Easter: they mean nothing to him, or so he says. Maybe they are too sore a reminder of the family life that he had known and lost. Maybe Angus's compact kitchen, compact discs and compact boat tell you all you need to know about a man who has everything he needs within reach but neither ritual nor ceremony in his life.

I asked him once whether he would be happier on solid ground, like everyone else. He says living on a boat gives you a different sort of freedom, makes you feel you can always go somewhere, even though *Verity* will never set sail. From one end comes the rumble of traffic, and from the other, the interference of the wind over the river, yet he claims rarely to notice the noise.

I say, 'I worry that you're lonely.'

We are lazing on the sofa, listening to the sounds of a spring evening. Sometimes, beyond the whirr of traffic and the hum of passing boats, you can hear the energetic call of a bird, for a mate. We have listened to Bon Jovi living on a prayer and giving love a bad name, whilst mapping out loosely what wrongs we would put right if either of us were Prime Minister. Now, I am lying with my head in Angus's lap, contemplating his early loss and how quietly life has turned out for him, his home un-peopled – hyphenated from the city by the small jetty that divides tarmac from water.

Staring into his whisky glass, he says, 'I wasn't lonely before, really. I am now, sometimes. When I miss you.'

He threads his fingers through my hair, and just as I did when he first told me about the accident, I feel the compelling tug of intimacy – an increase in the shared and confidential space we now inhabit. Bound by the truths he has told me, I am gentle with him. Over supper, I notice myself checking him as I would a child, for signs of malady. Yet when eventually we go to bed and he rises above me, ample with pleasure, I contract with pity and sorrow. Pain jabs at my insides but I do not tell him I will make it up to him. He is worth more than the lie I could tell – that I can compensate for his loss. So, I don't imply an intention to fill the gap left decades earlier. Instead, mute, I sustain my grip whilst he, collapsed and expended, mutters his allegiance into my neck. I hold him tightly, digging my fingers into his back. My elbows are compressed against his ribs and our skin is sticking together so that when we come to peel ourselves from one another it will sting. I reckon it's about the best I can do, for now.

Mel winds her arms around me from behind.

'Careful, darling. This pan's hot.'

'Are we going to school on our bikes today?'

'No, just our legs. We're walking.'

She puts her hands on the backs of my thighs, strokes them, says, 'You're warm.' I think of Angus, and how discriminating a body is in response to touch, depending upon the person who is touching it.

She says, 'You do need to get dressed, Mummy. You can't go to school in your pants and T-shirt.'

'Can't I?'

'Yuck! Embarrassing!'

I reach around to squeeze my daughter. She giggles and pats my bottom. She does not know she is reinstating herself: I have always been hers.

But while she and her sister are at school, I leave the house once more on Angus's account. I find privacy on flinty banks beside dormant cornfields. I plug my ears with music that belongs only to him and me and I replay our latest couplings in unison:

'Tell me.'

'I adore you.'

'Tell me again. Tell me anything.'

'I want you, I love you, I'm yours.'

Sounds. Sirens on the Embankment. A seagull screeching. The crackling of sheets and our breathing, afterwards – petty, shivering sighs.

I kiss his cheeks, eyes, mouth, throat, chest. I move down his body to where he is still sticky and wet, cooling now. He groans gently. I lick his stomach. Its surface is damp and salty but the skin sweet beneath.

'I could do it all over again.'

'So could I.' He pulls me upwards into his arms. 'If I were twenty years younger.'

'I'm so glad you're not.'

'I wish I were. I'm an old codger.'

'You're not, you're perfect. I love you so much.'

'Why did it take me sixty years to find you?'

'Why did it take me forty-two?'

'I don't ever want to lose you.'

'I don't ever want to be lost.'

'Except like this.'

'Except like this.'

One man, Rich, a Canadian marine scientist (special subject, plankton) – he was the one whose jokes I remember best, the one before Mark who came closest to filling me with a sense of possibility in a shared future. I remember his body very well. Naturally, I have never told Mark how well I remember the feel of Rich, but I do. I remember my delight when he first took off his clothes, and then mine. It took about thirty unequivocal seconds. I thought, *I could get completely lost in this man.* Naked, Rich was perfect: broad-shouldered, with a wide, strong chest and immense, powerful legs. He had colossal hands, too, which were burnished from working fishing boats for a year in order to earn the money to be here in the Himalayas with a misty view of Everest and an English girl. 'Except,' I said, 'I'm not really English.' He laughed, 'You could have fooled me!' He picked me up and carried me to the poorly sprung bed in the squalid hostel room where we were staying, and with joy and deliberation made me his own. I remained that way for almost three years – his. On and off, we lived and travelled together and though we made no big promises we loved one another as loyally as if we had. Finally, the Atlantic got between us, as we had always known it would. We understood that with marriage any minor differences between us would likely transmute to major, given a breach of some 3,600 miles for one person, so we avoided any serious discussion of it. Our end was sad but good-natured. I would have been amazed if it had been otherwise: it had been an auspicious beginning.

Rich came after a man whose shape was all wrong, someone I did not fit, who had no interest in the contours of my thoughts and laughed at things I found distasteful. I was on a train to Cornwall, heading to Sennen Cove to camp in the low dunes for the weekend with some friends. He was sitting in the seat opposite, a divorced BBC producer three decades older than me. He told me camping was forbidden on the beach. I said I knew that.

I liked the unanticipated nature of our meeting and I gambled with myself a lot more in those days, so we became a couple somehow, if only for five months. I loved his cottage tucked like a sheltering animal into the incline of a cove on the northern tip of West Penwith: it was romantic waking up somewhere so remote, where gannets dived and the wind blew so hard that the windows were salted murky-white. Staying with him in the Langham Hotel opposite Broadcasting House felt glamorous as well, in the days when the BBC thought nothing of putting up its long-distance staff in expensive hotels. I loved the high vulgarity of the place; the breakfasts and the miniature shower gels that came as a by-product of time spent with my suitor. He was also very good-looking. What can I say? I was young. I thought I rocked.

It was reasonably disastrous from the outset. Already impossibly jaded for his age, Trevelyan (for this was his name) was dismissive of the world into which I, aged eighteen, was just venturing. Trevelyan loathed my enthusiasm and had no defences against it save to belittle the things I held dear, and the people, too. When I introduced him to my friends it was clear he despised them, and they him. It wasn't even a relationship I could later justify by saying, 'Well, at least the sex was good,' because it wasn't, it was terrible.

My friends thought I was nuts. No one understood what I was doing with such a nervy, graceless admirer (only much later did I wonder what the hell a man of forty-eight was doing picking up an A-level student on a train). His jealousy sapped me, his possessiveness, also: if I so much as acknowledged another male he would fume and sulk until he could take me to bed to reclaim me. Worse, he never stopped telling me how much he admired my father's work.

I might have stood for it had the relationship had any imaginative intensity but it did not. Yet for a good year, give or take, Trevelyan continued to write long letters explaining how his devotion would nourish my uncertainty. His attention could have been interesting, even in the most negative of ways, but it was not, and curiously, like a persistent virus, it was difficult to recover from. The ennui he induced drained me of colour for some time afterwards. Rich was the best possible retort. Only six years older than me, his home was a shabby shack on a fir-covered promontory above a beach on the Newfoundland coast. He made his own furniture and caught his own supper. He kayaked to work. He saw the world for what it might be, not for what he had already decided it was. He was refreshing, in all senses.

I say Trevelyan drained me of colour but I have only myself to blame. Apart from the initial surprise of his Cornish name and the allure of his chiselled features there was nothing about him that made me catch my breath, so what I was doing with him God only knows, except that teenage vanity can be a ferociously potent driving force, especially if conflated with the impassioned Atlantic elements. Now, I know it was the ocean and the seabirds that kept me so long on that highly charged stretch of Cornish coast: drenched in sensation, I was busy claiming my life as my own; believing myself possible.

Mark comes in later and later. I have usually eaten with the girls and put them to bed by the time he enters the kitchen and finds me sitting at the table, my laptop open. I tilt the screen down to a forty-five-degree angle and he says things like, 'It's a classic midlife crisis, this thing of yours: you do realize that?' I indicate the food I cooked earlier, in which he shows scant interest. He makes himself coffee. I wait. When he leaves the room, I unfold the screen, continue where I left off.

I calculate. I am forty-two. Twice that is eighty-four. It is hard to argue, statistically, that I am not in more or less midlife, or thereabouts. But crisis? When taking my daughters to school, I run ahead and pounce out from behind hedges to surprise them; and at suppertimes, I carve silly faces in their mashed potato. My husband never wants for clean, folded T-shirts. At any given point, there are two bottles of laundry liquid and a spare roll of bin-liners between me and poor husbandry. I am not in crisis.

I think of my mother, for whom a well-stocked cupboard meant nothing. When she was the age I am now, she was buried in an abundance of data on the incidence of Aids and HIV in the UK's hetero-sexual population. When Mark's mother, Jane, was forty-two, she was buried in the ground of a Wiltshire churchyard.

I'm sorry I never knew Jane, not just for obvious

reasons but because I feel that Mark might make better sense to me if I had. A mother is key to a man, and whilst I had managed to find a way in to Mark I was not quite sure how I had got there, or why.

There are photographs, of course. Impassive, Jane stands formally dressed beside her husband David in his army uniform, or in family clusters, her hands to her sides, touching no one in particular; necessary to the group but not critically bound to it. There are plenty of pictures of her with Mark and his older brother Philip and in those she looks suitably proud. As for her wedding photograph, like most wedding photographs it could be anyone's. If her expression suggests anything specific you might say she looks untried, and by that I don't mean virginal; I mean that she looks as more people should on their wedding day, like a new recruit at the beginning of a long posting, with a fitting degree of enthusiasm for what lies ahead but no concept of what that might be.

I've been told she enjoyed walking and that she read a bit, Thomas Hardy and Dickens. I know she was well brought up, sensible, quiet, not given to colourful self-expression. I understand she took Mark's deafness and David's lengthy, worrying spells in Belfast and Kosovo in her stride. Whether that crucial third dimension, life's breath itself, would have enabled Jane to shed any more light on her younger son for me I will never know, although I wonder occasionally whether Mark's more oblique aspects derive from her. I can only see my husband's mother as I imagine her: a person who disclosed little of herself before withdrawing unobtrusively from a life devoid of spectacle or personal request. But maybe that is fancy on my part.

'No, you're not far off. That's pretty much what she was like.'

'Don't you ever wonder, though,' I asked Mark, early on, 'whether she was mysterious or passionate underneath? That perhaps there was more there than you saw when you were a child and teenager.'

'I really don't think so.'

'Unlike your dad.'

'Definitely unlike Dad.'

David after Jane: a man with his life turned upside down (quite literally if you take into account the geography) and translated into something warmer, a second act set in a luscious, subtropical garden a short salt-breeze from the beach. He moved to Australia before I met Mark and during the times we've spent together I've come to like him well enough although I prefer his second wife, Lindsay, with her red-blooded, no-nonsense Aussie-ness. A pincher of cheeks and ruffler of hair, Lindsay's fingernails are scarlet and glossy, her perfume is gorgeous and her rounded body abundant in denim shorts and men's floating white shirts. Her fridge is a carnival of taste and colour, stocked with beer, pastrami, and strawberry tarts, and when her teenage grandchildren from her first marriage come to visit she invites them to help themselves to its pleasure-inducing contents before pursuing them around the shrubbery with the garden hose. She maintains a convivial, if merciless, atmosphere – something so redolent of the British military it is unsurprising that David finds marriage to her as agreeable to him as life in the army. However, Lindsay's real talent is not pricking relentlessly at her husband's taut Englishness but knowing exactly the moment to desist, so that whenever her caustic, Antipodean mockery threatens to overwhelm David, she winds her arm around his neck, kisses it sumptuously, and calls him a silly old bugger. I have always thought it would be delicious to be loved by Lindsay if you were a man: she would provide such a soft-scented, pillowy retreat. If you were an uptight English brigadier, your career concluded and your first wife dead, you could do a lot worse than wind up in Lindsay's frank embrace. You might even consider yourself the luckiest man in the southern hemisphere.

Mark and I visited them once when the twins were little but the flight was a nightmare. It's a hell of a long and expensive way to go for a bucket-and-spade holiday with the grandparents, and I wouldn't let the girls play freely in the garden because earlier that month Lindsay had come across not one but two King Browns in the shrubbery. 'Great lifestyle!' everyone chimed. 'Great lifestyle!' But I wasn't into checking flower beds for deadly reptiles or risk-assessing the car's sun visors for venomous spiders. The heat was fierce and the climate as unforgiving as the social politics. I had never been anywhere so hostile. (The beaches were nice.)

We have no plans to return and it's a shame in a way because Lindsay's someone I can talk to. I have happy memories of our three-year-old daughters in the curvature of her sun-stippled garden spray, begging for mercy and ice creams. David used to come to England every year to see Mark and his older brother Philip, then every eighteen months, but that has stretched to every two years. He and Lindsay are getting on a bit now and long-haul flights take their toll on ageing bodies and army pensions.

When I ask Mark if he ever wishes his father had stayed home, retired instead into his native land and character, he says no. He says it wouldn't have made any difference.

'Why not?'

'He was around so little when I was growing up that any geographical distance between us is academic, really. It was always Mum.'

Mark was fifteen when Jane died. David was serving in Northern Ireland at the time and only when the cancer was so advanced that his wife's chin was receding into her jaw, did David come home and stay home. It was quick. Mark was at boarding school with Philip, insulated from nothing, but David thought it best the boys stay put for as long as possible. They joined him for their mother's last five days, helping to turn her in bed, repulsed by the feel of her spine through her nightdress, numbed into wordlessness by her reduction. Mark says they were appalled by the sores around her mouth, the few remaining wilted hairs on her puckered skull, skin like parchment; by how much she had withered. Rheumy-eyed, her fingers were comic-strip scrawny, her gums prominent, ugly.

Betrayed, Mark retreated. He put his head down and worked. By the time he gained a place at Oxford he realized he had become so unsociable that quite apart from anything else his lip-reading skills were very slightly compromised. He needed new mouths in his life to keep him sharp. He had no choice: necessity demanded gregariousness. He willed himself to make new friends, went to parties – excruciating though he found them – and chatted up women. In close corners of gloomy pubs and ill-lit college rooms he hung on their every word and they, charmed by his rapt attention, fell in love with him in their numbers. But Mark was not besotted himself, he was simply concentrating on seeing what they had to say, a pursuit made more demanding by the lack of decent light to be found in a city comprised of old buildings with small windows. He even made a point, that first year at least, of singling out foreign students for his best attention. Apart from the thrill of sexual variety he badly needed the practice with accents – or so he claims.

The greatest challenge came from the East; India and Iran, specifically. He tells me French and German women were a form of light relief by comparison. Scandinavians were pretty clear, the Dutch a little more challenging, but as Mark put it to me once, 'Who cares about talking when there's a pair of legs in your bed that are longer than the bed itself?' Americans were easiest of all to understand, easier sometimes than the English: the English too often give up speech reluctantly, like a secret. Americans, Mark insists, have it all going on out front. They don't swallow their words, don't keep them all to themselves.

Mark broke a lot of hearts over the ensuing years, for the pattern of easy non-loving that he developed whilst a student remained in place for a long while. A couple of times in his early thirties he made an effort to settle into something regular with attractive, friendly women but he didn't find it easy. Jane's premature death had doubtless made him wary of binding himself conclusively to another human being but if her demise had confined him further than he was already confined by his deafness, it was his independence – a harsh self-reliance required in order to cope in a silent world – that made him so in-accessible in the first instance. To survive in solitary confinement, let alone prosper, demands levels of discipline and self-belief not required of many people and in working so hard to be ordinary, Mark made himself exceptional.

Interestingly, people took it as read. They did not understand that instead of being straightforwardly lavished with talents Mark was compelled to obscure his impairment with hard-won achievements. His memory and scrupulous attention to detail were legendary among those who knew him but few people realized that he had his own techniques and contrivances, developed in childhood when it became clear that without that crucial fifth sense it was going to be much harder for him to remember things than it was for those who could hear. Deprived of the recollective clues with which sound is suffused, all the triggers and insinuations, the myriad hints and prompts, Mark's dependence on alternative reminders was considerable. Anything that might prove a useful aide-memoire for the future was recorded by him in a small notebook or scribbled on Post-it notes that were stuck, hopeful as religious petitions at a shrine, to the walls of his studio. It didn't much matter what it was – whether a place visited, a person met or an idea procured – Mark, clerk-like, would document it. He does so still to this day, not in order to chronicle the passing of time but so he may be able reliably to refer backwards in order to avoid admitting, when a memory needs retrieving, 'I can't remember because I didn't hear it.' That, he insists, would feel like the admission, 'I never remember because I'm not really whole.' And fuck that.

What anyone else made of Mark's younger self, a persona so assiduously shaped by private resolve and concealed methods, the man himself could not afford to care, preferring to be defined by determination rather than by the deafness he sought so determinedly to overcome. If people considered Mark extraordinary despite his deafness instead of being extraordinary partly as a result of it, that was good enough for him.

All of this had its downside, though. While Mark's tenacity set him apart, in an ironic twist of fate the more he strove to prove himself in no way lacking, the more he came to be regarded as having an indecent excess of good fortune: talent, brains, looks, wit. This aroused envy in others, and not a little distrust, either. In addition, his commitment to keeping his appreciable exertions hidden beneath a carapace of effortlessness lent him an air of inviolability, so whilst his admirers thought him charismatic and charming his detractors took him for a smooth git: they thought him slippery and impregnable, a bit of a tosser; conceited.

In no area of his life did Mark invoke more resentment than in his treatment of women. Not only did he garner them with ease but he maintained their fascination as well as any of his male contemporaries, and with almost no inconvenience to himself. He became adept at sustaining a lot of ankle-deep relationships at once and professed not to understand why the women he slept with minded so much the lack of depth. He promised them nothing, was his reasoning. Certainly, he had enormous appeal. His jawline was strong, his skin smooth, his eyes long-lashed and the dark, near-shoulder-length curls he had grown in order to conceal his hearing aids enhanced his natural sexiness. He was clever and punctilious and made people laugh. By the time he was painting seriously, in spattered Levi's and large checked shirts, the way he looked, combined with the stacked canvases, tubes of oils and the reek of paint that suffused everything he possessed, lent him a compellingly romantic quality that even his darker characteristics could not easily dispel.

He was also, and crucially, flattering to a fault. He gave each of his girlfriends a nickname and remembered details about their mothers or little brothers – even their childhood pets. He could recall their favourite foods, the music that had meaning for them (even though the latter usually meant nothing to him), and the various reasons why their last relationships did not work out. He was highly plausible. They didn't know that Mark remembered people's personal details because he had trained himself to. (After all, there are probably only so many times you can ask someone to repeat themselves before they may stop wanting to see you any more.) As a result, they felt uniquely cared for.

They were anything but. Mark appreciated diversity but offered special treatment to no one. He was never mean – at least, that's what he says now, and it's probably true if you're being loose with the word: he has admitted to being neglectful and deliberately evasive, but overtly mean? This he denies, though not forcefully. I tell him that evasion is mean and there is such a thing as cruelty by omission, too, but he says that not a lot of single men subscribe willingly to that notion, at least not when they are young, and he was no exception: being called a fucking lying, shallow bastard once in a while seemed a small price to pay for unlimited personal attention. Therefore, his door was always open, even if his heart was not, and because he found the company of women so agreeable, some took it to mean he might be disposed to love them. When he made it clear that this was unlikely, the sensible ones disappeared to find a better bet.

Others, whose devotion superseded their good sense, lingered to see if they could persuade the bastard otherwise. Disinclined to turn down all of his girlfriends outright, Mark listened to their coaxing and inducements. He invited them back into his bed and they accepted, relieved, for briefly they believed that he had registered their longing and distress and was touched. Yet while he upheld a relaxed and jocular atmosphere, he was palpably unmoved. Ultimately, his cheerfulness was a rebuke too far. 'Don't cry!' he would plead, for almost inevitably they did, understanding at last that even the most carefully played-out reunions did not signify hope for a future. Most men are exasperated by tears but the main reason Mark shrinks from the lachrymose is because he can't lip-read mouths distorted by sorrow. Still, cry they mostly did. A couple threw things at him in frustration, or so I gather. Another even punched him in the jaw. One woman, Greek I think, went the extra mile and kicked a hole in a canvas. Later, she sent photos of her wedding. 'Oh, my God!' said Mark, as the bride emerged resplendent from a creamy envelope embossed with the new family name. 'I remember her!'

When I asked him once, 'Why me?' he replied as if I'd asked him something as incontrovertible as whether night follows day: 'Because I love you.'

When I said that there is always more to love than love, he said he liked the fact that I didn't beat about the bush: I wanted him, I let him know and I made it clear from the beginning that unless he felt the same way in return I wasn't going to stay for breakfast – so to speak.

'It focuses the mind, that. From day one, I knew I didn't want to lose you. I'd never felt that way before. Also, you have a lot of energy. You want that in a wife. No man wants a passenger, he wants a co-pilot.'

Mark didn't ask me what it was about him. He didn't feel the need to, I suppose.

'Don't you want to know?' I enquired. 'What it is about you?'

We were lying around in bed, warm and lazy, the duvet rippled. He pulled me into his embrace.

'Go on, then,' he said.

'I trust that you will never let me down.'

He kissed my forehead.

'And I won't.'

And he hasn't.

I am in a mood for disposal. I move through my home, seeking out the ropiest pairs of shoes, single socks, broken toys, ill-fitting underwear, chipped plates. I fill bin-bags with old clothes. As a police officer might seize the opportunity to bust a criminal skulking in a dank lock-up, I fall upon the bucket beneath the kitchen sink. 'Aha!' I say. 'Your time is up.'

I bought that bucket when Mark and I married – I recall its purchase very clearly. I remember thinking that buying a bucket to put beneath the kitchen sink was a totem of married life if anything was. Now, I decide, it has seen better days. *Like us*, I think – and then I stop myself. Maybe not like us, after all.

I drop the bags of clothes at the village recycling bins. The bin for paper and card is overflowing. Trodden into the ground beside it a popular TV actor smiles broadly from the straggling pages of a tabloid newspaper. *'Nation's favourite'*. *'A household name'*. He has been cavorting for twenty years with a cadre of prostitutes in a basement in Paddington, and one of them has decided it's time to let everyone know that he likes it in the dark and he loves to be punished; the weirder, the better. Without even bending down, I can read that his wife has gone into hiding: she is photographed leaving the £1.75-million family home, looking hunted. She is in the dark now, feeling punished. Friends of the couple testify to his devotion: *'She's his rock,'* says one. *'He's beside himself.'*

Beside himself. I picture the actor split in two – his alter ego always elsewhere, wanting to be free, wanting to be sequestered – and I wonder what difference there is between him and me. My desire for Angus may not be hidden from my spouse but many would judge it freakish or unacceptable, the way I crawl into the dark of *Verity*'s hull, into Angus's creaky old bed. He may not dangle me from the ceiling with chains, or whip me into a frenzy with God knows what implements but perhaps my falling asleep tight in his grip is equally treacherous.

It is possible that if people knew, some might be sympathetic. Many have troubles of their own. Some would see me differently, and an unhappy few would relish their own lack of charity: the world can be unmerciful, with its carping and its ready judgements, and even amongst friends there are those who are always ready to see someone else's dream tainted. Most, I am sure, wouldn't care. Among those who might care, there would be some for whom I would be a disappointment – for not being quite the person they believed me to be; for causing them to stop and take stock. What we do causes others to reassess.

A mother from school is posting crushed plastic milk bottles. She says, 'You've had a good clear-out by the looks of it.'

The manager of the village shop wants to know where I've been hiding: 'I haven't seen you in ages. I was beginning to think you'd deserted us.'

'I'd never do that.'

'Only kidding,' she says.

A good clear-out. I wonder, often these days, whether I have become part of the general destruction of something much bigger than myself. I, with a husband and children, a job of sorts, a clean driving licence and no criminal record: am I, along with the drug-dealers and teenage fathers and every other subgroup that society cares to blame, just as responsible for its breakdown? I bet I am the only woman in the village doing this. I don't know that for sure but I would put good money on it – like the gambler that I seem to have become; overspending on pleasure, notching up debt after debt, knowing that one day I will have to pay but for now there is Angus, warm salve to my troubled spirit. Maybe if my presence cannot be counted upon in my local shop, let alone the marital home, I am undermining something reliable in the community to which I surely bear some responsibility. Perhaps I am tugging, bit by bit, at the tiniest threads of other people's social fabric, destroying, indiscriminately, things that are whole. It makes me feel sick, to think about.

Every instinct I have is telling me to stay at home. I ignore them all. I move in a straight line for Angus and nothing stands in my way. I cook meals, wash clothes, confirm dates with existing clients, answer questions from potential ones ('Do you do pets?' 'It depends. Not reptiles.'). There is always more required of me but at some point, I walk past the remaining demands, like a soldier through the debris of warfare, and make my way towards Angus. I am possessed by the desire to be with him. There is nothing to my left, nothing right.

Reason crumbles. Habits fall away. In the light of the open fridge door, naked at 2 a.m., Angus falls upon a chocolate cake I brought with me – purchased at school on a Fundraising Friday and made by Sandra, mother of Chloe in Year One.

'"May contain nuts,"' he reads. 'Right up your street then, saucy girl!'

Who's to say where and when cake should be eaten, and in what circumstances? Nonetheless, I feel as if something has been defiled.

'I love this,' Angus says, and I don't really know if he means me and him or just the chocolate cake. When I try some, it sticks to my teeth. I hate myself.

My absences from the twins seem to me so inexcusable that in my attempts to compensate all manner of things improve. The quality of my attention wavers less. I listen to what they have to tell me. I invest more in the games we play and the stories I read to them at bedtime. I cook better and with more care and invite their friends to play at the weekends. When they drop glitter on the carpet I do not chide. The fuller I am of Angus, the greater my commitment to anything that may disprove evidence of his impact on our lives. The more profound my shame, the less I criticize Mark. These by-products of my remorse keep me busy. I am so convinced of my delinquency that I will do anything. I sign up weeks ahead to run a stall at the school fete. Conspicuous effort is my only redress, tenderness my reparation.

It fails to unite my two halves. On the day of the fete

– and surely because a school event is one place he really should not be – Angus is on a loop in my mind, raising himself beside me on his bed, pulling me gently up and towards him, settling his body on to mine: up and over; hold; pause. Hold. Pause. I wonder at the loveliness of Angus's face as he looks down into mine. I am in thrall to its contrasts, to its cragginess and finer features. It is a face that is getting old but to me it is beautiful still: the lines around his mouth are deep, like ravines in silk.

A man carrying a baby asks me for one orange juice and two raisin muffins. Angus is still looking at me. I am here and I am there, and how both places feel authentically my own I do not understand, but they do. Even so, as I serve soft drinks and cakes to familiar people in a bunting-swathed playground, I am aware as never before that not one of them knows who I really am. I give the man his change, in twenty-pence pieces. I smile at the baby. I feel like a secret in plain sight, invisible and exposed. My head swims, back to the boat. Sometimes, I lie with my nose so close to Angus's skin that it is hard to breathe properly. I love the way the smell of him cancels out everything else. I want it to. I remember how much of the twins' first weeks I spent inhaling them. Nuzzling their round, furry heads, I couldn't get enough of whatever primal scent it is that so captivates new mothers. But it faded eventually, the magnetic aroma of the young and fresh; it faded and there was nothing I could do to preserve its essence. Some people say it's like being unable to smell your own home, the way you cannot readily verify your own family: you are part of it, so how could you expect to identify it as separate? On the other hand, what would you do if cast into the wild? Animals detect their kin by sniffing them out but could I locate Mark and the girls by scent alone? Is this what partly draws us to others, I wonder? The heady provocation and enticement of a new aroma that will reawaken our senses and make our skin prickle – reminding us of the animals we are? Angus smells of soap and aftershave and the resolute warmth of his body. But I have ceased to be able to smell Mark. When did that happen? I cannot tell. I can still bury my face in the twins' hair and know where I belong but the scent of Mark has assumed neutrality as if my nose, like my heart, is recalibrating itself. I remember Angus making clear to me, not the first time together but maybe the second or third, exactly what he wanted: 'Breathe me,' he insisted. 'Make me us.' I recall feeling flattered, required and alarmed.

Ways of coping with the fear develop and become ingrained. On journeys back from *Verity*, I reassemble myself. As if I were a player switching costumes for the next scene, the train has become my place of transformation. I shower and change before leaving but on the train the ritual of cleansing and rearrangement is internalized. Always, I sit facing the direction of travel, make a point of taking in the view as I get closer to home; and though trains lend themselves perfectly to reflection, I do not reflect. I do not dare. I have become too frightened by how quickly my life recedes the minute I turn the car off our yard and on to the single-track road into town. I am scared that even as I leave I am already elsewhere, the train journey merely a migratory passage, of the flesh. Which is why, returning, I banish all thoughts of Angus and allow a hollowness to settle upon me. I stare out of the window, unseeing. Fertile hedges streak past and I fail to register them. If it rains I do not care. When the sky clears, I barely notice the division of the clouds.

Time has begun to lose its meaning. At 7 p.m. on a school night, Angus drives us through London's expensive, antiseptic heart. I'd be happiest on the boat going nowhere but he wants to treat us to a restaurant. I tell him it's May, it's warm enough to eat on deck, on *Verity* – but he replies, 'I've thought of that, nutcase, and booked a table outside, on the terrace.'

I never get this time again.

Mark is always saying that. He says it to the twins when they are fighting. He says it in traffic jams. He says it when he has explained three times by email to his mobile phone provider why he doesn't want to pay for five hundred minutes of free calls a month because, being deaf, he has no need of them.

I will never get this weekend again. Or more accurately, I will never get to spend it with my children: I have given it away, to someone else, and they will never have it. It will not be part of their childhood store of their mother.

Angus does not know how homesick London makes me. I look out of the car window. Street after street of halogen-lit boutiques adorned with things that shine. I search for evidence of normality until somewhere amongst the couture and jewellery shops I spot a small sign for a hospice – the clearest of reminders that real life exists beyond this assembly of decadent emporia, and is precarious. Quite suddenly, in my slinky dress, one hand resting on Angus's thigh, I miss the twins with such intensity that my throat constricts. I think about taking them to the GP when they were very small, each with a fever and rash, both of them pink and tetchy. The advice dispensed was sensible, predictable: *Calpol and rest, wait and see, come back if it persists.* It persisted. Their rashes worsened. They vomited and shivered and were difficult to hydrate. Nauseous with fear, I rolled glass tumblers over the spots on their backs and outlined with felt-tip the blotches on their thighs so that I could chart the progress of their rashes. I resisted A&E but a bag was packed and ready. Mark was halfway up a Scottish mountain at the time, painting cloud formations in a rented croft with no Wi-Fi: texts and emails outlining my insomniac near-derangement went unanswered. When he reappeared a week later, the twins were full of post-viral ennui – sporadically active, then listless and irritable. 'See,' he said, 'you didn't need me anyway. They're fine. You're such a good mummy.'

Now, as Angus negotiates a road diversion – 'Christ, we'd be better off walking!' – I see Miranda on her side, thumb in her mouth, damp-haired after a bath. I want to walk into her bedroom this minute: I want to stroke her forehead and lift her plump arm to my mouth and kiss it, savour the softness of her skin. Melanie sleeps on her back, arms slung across the duvet. At six, she is already becoming long-limbed: one day, I know, she will be inviting to other people, in other ways. I do not want to imagine it.

'Sweetheart,' murmurs Angus, and he turns his head slightly towards me, having extricated us from a tangle of one-way streets and located a parking space, 'you look so very lovely tonight.' And it is probably the effect of Angus swinging the car around all those right-angled bends but I feel nauseous. I smile, wanly, and my lover smiles back, broadly, his face crumpled with pleasure, convinced by the here and now. Angus's faith in the present differs from mine.

In bed, he sings into the back of my neck, '"Birds flyin' high, you know how I feel . . ."'

'I was asleep.'

'Okay, "Goldfinger . . . He's the man, the man with the Midas touch . . ."'

'Be quiet.'

He says, 'I can't believe we have a whole weekend together.'

'What time is it?'

'Good heavens, it's exactly midnight.'

I squeeze myself backwards into the curve of him.

'I'm hungry!' he announces. 'I'm always hungry when I've eaten out. Mouse portions, it's absurd.' He kneads me gently in the hip. 'How about you?' Without waiting for a response, he disentangles himself and springs out of bed.

'Come on!' he calls back down the stairs. 'Lots of good things up here!'

In the kitchen, I put on his large cook's apron before sitting down at the table.

'Mmmm, kinky!' he murmurs. 'But you won't be needing that.'

'I will. It's the only item of clothing in this room and I'm starkers.'

'Precisely,' says Angus. 'Just as the Almighty intended.' He makes his way to the table, a bottle of Famous Grouse under one arm, a pair of tumblers in one hand, and a circular wooden board in the other: upon it is some

geological-looking fruit cake and a strapping chunk of
Stilton. A knife with a curved blade lies to one side of the
cheese. He sits down heavily, opposite me.

'Here we go,' he announces. 'Midnight snack.'

I eye the provisions with some concern.

'That's not a snack, it's an expedition survival kit. Can I
be honest with you?'

'Please.'

'I hate Stilton, I hate fruit cake and I hate whisky.'

'You hate whisky?'

'Paint stripper.'

'Oh, my darling, a woman agin both jazz and Scotch.
This is not looking promising.' He cuts a broad wedge of
cheese for himself and blows me a kiss. 'Thank heavens
we've found a mutual love of something else.' Frowning
at the apron, which is hanging limply down my front, he
says, 'Take that thing off. I want to look at you.'

I comply.

'Ah. How much better that is. What would you like
instead?'

'Nothing. Sleep. And that's a fish knife you're using for
the cheese.'

'So it is.' He hums, frowns, says, 'I'm thinking some
tinned pears would go nicely with this.'

'I'm cold.'

'Come with me.' He takes my hand. 'I can fix that in
a jiffy.'

Beside the sofa, he wraps me in a rug that he takes from the basket on the floor, and a pale blue jersey that has been squashed beneath it, reveals itself. 'Aha!' he says. 'I've been looking for this!' He pulls it over his head. 'And it's long enough to cover my vitals, too. Marvellous. You sit down, angel. I'll be back.'

I don't sit. I wander around, looking out across the river at the lights in the buildings opposite, and inside, at Angus's sheet music on the piano: Chopin's Minute Waltz; Mozart's Sonata No 16 in C major; Debussy's Clair de Lune. He has a private recital coming up in a fortnight, in Bath. I scrutinize the only framed photograph on the entire boat, of a tall, teenage Angus standing between his parents in a garden – theirs; his. I screw up my eyes but it is impossible to make out as clearly as I want to the finer features of the man and woman flanking him. I pick up a couple of postcards, lying along the top of some books in the long shelves, and read the messages on their reverse sides. *'Thanks so much for a lovely supper and evening. Anna.'* *'Dearest A, Brilliant to see you, as always. Love, S.'* Anna has signed off with one kiss, S with two.

Angus reappears with a bowl of tinned pears. He sets them down on the low table beside the sofa and says through a mouthful of cake, 'What you got there, sweetheart?'

'Missives from your ex-girlfriends, I think.'

He takes the cards from me, flips them over.

'Nah. This one's a colleague from the Royal College, married. And this one's a very old friend.'

'S?'

'Sarah. We're just mates. We went to bed for the summer about forty years ago but we never made a proper go of anything. She's a violinist with the LSO, also married. You should meet her sometime; you'd like each other.'

I think, *All this life he has had before me.*

'My darling girl,' Angus asks, 'are you jealous? You've no need to be.'

'Don't be so ridiculous.'

'You are!' He throws back his head and laughs. 'Oh, nutcase, how sweet! And over an old chubster like me, too; how very gratifying.' He slings one arm around me and with his other one, stretches across to some CDs in the shelves. 'You're the love of my life,' he says. 'You know that.'

'I've come so late in the day, though.'

'If you'd come into my life when I was twenty-five, I'd have been down on one knee without a second thought.'

'I was seven.'

'Thirty-five, then. Forty-five. Whenever.' He kisses the top of my head. 'What shall we listen to?'

'You choose.'

'Okay,' he says, 'lucky dip.' He pulls out a CD. 'Ah,

Vivaldi!' he declares, as if he has run unexpectedly into an old friend in the street. 'How lovely!'

Mark will be at home with the girls, sleeping.

Angus inserts the CD into the player and sings the opening along with the soprano: '*Nulla in mundo pax sincera . . .*' He says, as if emerging from a trance, 'God, it's beautiful. And she ain't lyin', nutcase. No true peace in this world, indeed.'

From the ambit of his arms, I say, 'That photo of you with your parents.'

'Yes.'

'Is it the last one ever taken of the three of you?'

'It is.' He pauses. 'This man is an island. Population: one delectable woman.'

I think, *You can't say that. I am another country, and I am already fully populated. You can't just colonize me.*

'What's wrong?'

I think, *I am not who you think I am. The me that you love is an adaptation of someone else. I am just a version of her, happening to you.*

'Nothing's wrong.'

'If you say so.'

He smiles and lowers his eyes, and there is something about his expression that, quite suddenly, I do not approve of – a bashfulness I have not seen before that does not strike me as entirely authentic – and I realize that I must never feel sorry for Angus, for sympathy works like a hook. Even my mother – her marriage to my father a complicated exercise in compromise – never submitted to my father's entreaties for reassurance, whether overt or otherwise, and I am certain the devotion she engendered in him was due in no small part to this. I could see, when I was growing up, that she was without question the deepest and most enduring of his passions, yet even to him she retained sufficient distance that his desire for her never really waned. Her ease in male company may also have contributed to my father's sense of his wife as the jewel in his crown. There was something about her that made men behave like small boys, as if she were a puzzle in the room they all wanted to solve. She was perfectly happy for them to feel that way, and so was my father, for he was the one to whom this singular woman was married; the one with whom she went home. Never mind that he was well-known and polished. My mother was cleverer than my father, difficult to instruct and impossible to perturb. A man knows when he's in luck and my father knew not to push his.

I never wanted to feel the way my father did: I never wished simultaneously to endure, as he so clearly did, the longing for a loved one and the loss of self – and self-respect – that went with it. *It is terrible to love and not possess: it is terrible to possess and not to love.* Someone said that, or wrote it, and during my father's manic phases, when two dozen roses were not enough, when only emerald earrings would do, or an impromptu trip to Florence, unbidden and ill-timed, I witnessed his deflation as my mother did her best to show appreciation. That she wished quietly to be left alone was obvious; and yet she adored my father, and understood perfectly his need to demonstrate to her as extravagantly as possible his copious love. Growing up, I observed it all and promised myself that in union with a man I would never put myself in either of my parents' positions.

It left its mark on me and Ed, being so rarely the targets of our parents' affections. Their love flew like arrows over our heads, missing us, and in the end, I held my father largely responsible: I was convinced that it was my mother's time-consuming management of him that apprehended her and kept her detached from my brother and me, from who we were and what made us tick. Ed fared better overall: he was absorbed into music, and my mother, the frustrated pianist who studied epidemiology only when it became clear she would never make the concert-hall platform herself, found a way into the soul of her son, and he into hers.

With Mark, I swore I would keep my distance, having learned early on the trick of surviving alongside a compelling man: want him less than he wants you; or appear to, anyway. I never wanted to feel responsible for a partner's happiness, I was well aware of the potential for failure – so when Angus asks, as our time together draws to a close,

'Do you think you will always love me?', instead of registering a straightforward request for reassurance from a man in love with a woman, I hear a bereaved child, whose needs no adult can meet. And rather than folding my arms around Angus with whom I am so much in love, and whispering heartfelt, amorous solace – and I wish I could, for I want to, I really want to be the kind of woman who can at any given time and without argument or defence offer ready consolation to a man – I reply, 'Not if you ask me questions like that.' And for that alone, never mind all my other defects and indiscretions, I despise myself.

'Okay. Apart from no kids, lots of time and a musical boat –' Mark says 'musical boat' as if something sour has got into his mouth, and I picture *Verity* on high seas, rising and falling to a symphonic swell – 'what the hell does he have that I don't?'

'Those are not the reasons why I like his company.'

'Really? Then I assume he's bloody magnificent in the sack.'

'I've told you already, it's not about the sex.'

'And what am I supposed to think about that? I mean, you and I don't have any, and you've never been especially drawn to celibacy.'

'Please!'

'Please what? Look, you can't just tell me it's not about the sex and think that makes it all okay.'

'I don't.'

'All right, so if I accept what you're saying, it must mean that something else is lacking here, for you.'

'Nothing's lacking.'

'It must be, otherwise you wouldn't be going elsewhere.'

'But it isn't. It's not a case of either/or. What I have with Angus is totally different.'

'Clearly.'

'It doesn't take anything away. In a strange way it augments—'

'Augments?!'

'Yes.'

'Yeah? Augments what, exactly?'

'What I mean is, if anything, now that I feel more—'

But I can't do it. I can't easily explain that moments with Angus do not equate to moments with the family because they bear no relation to it. The two kinds of experience can't be weighed or measured against one another because they're not made of the same material. A ton of feathers and a ton of lead weigh the same but even when you learn about things falling at equal speeds in a vacuum you know it's not the point because we don't live in vacuums. Feathers and lead dropped from a high-rise building will have a significantly different impact on anything below: a child could tell you that. No one would think to compare the two, except as opposites.

Mark says, 'Come on. Now that you feel more what?'

'Nothing.'

'Say it!'

'Loved.'

He stares at me. Then he says, 'Is that supposed to make me feel better?'

Suddenly, I am angry.

'It's not about you, Mark! Not everything is about you, okay? Not everything is about making life easier for you, softer for you, better for you! I'm fed up with trying to do that and getting sweet nowhere for myself. So yes, I feel loved. And yes, I love him. And yes, I feel less alone. Wanted, not needed. I feel met, not bypassed.'

'Bypassed? Jesus!'

'Yes. He's so open. I can talk to him about anything. Anything. He's just so warm.'

'Right.'

'Sorry. I'm sorry, I could have put it better.'

'No, I think you put it very clearly.'

'I'm just trying to answer your question.'

He says, 'Oh, I think you've done that.'

'And?'

He turns to leave.

'And nothing. I hear what you're saying.'

* * *

We married pretty fast, Mark and I. It took less than eight months to get out from under the cherry tree in our friend's garden to a honeymoon in Turkey, where the card on the king-sized bed addressed to Mr and Mrs Burdett, and the bowl of brightly coloured fruit decorated with a creamy silken ribbon, signalled our fresh pledges.

We agreed we would live abroad for a couple of years. Mark would paint and I would photograph, and when we came back to England we would set up our home. And so, we played Bohemia in southern France – I spoke the language, after all – though we were neither frivolous nor lazy, and we did a lot of work. The rent from Mark's flats meant we had just enough both to live on and pay the rent for a one-room apartment near the sea, and whenever there was enough money in our account, Mark had his paintings sent back to a gallery in London. I had managed to secure an agreement with a picture agency, and although I was only paid for my photographs once a third party requested them from the agency, I felt at last like a pro, if a penurious one: 'pitiful' was the word Mark used once, to describe my income. He meant it supportively, he said; he felt I was worth so much more. 'I've been paid!' I would whoop, when the agency phoned to say a photograph had been sold, which meant a royalty for me. 'That's my girl,' he'd reply. Then, 'Are we in single or double figures this time?'

When we were not working, we washed our dusty

clothes, swam in the sea, read books and played chess. I learned to gut fish and Mark taught himself to juggle with spoons and plait my hair. But we fought, and hard. Our styles differed. Mark was so partial to the high ground I had little choice but to occupy the low. When he was carelessly undermining, I would fly off the handle: a lofty aside from him – a remark as light as air – could produce an avalanche of invective from me. If he protested that my denunciation outweighed the original sin, I would berate him further: 'It's not just that you're a condescending wanker. You're a condescending wanker who's never learned when it's wise to keep quiet.' To which he replied, 'If I had the wit to keep quiet, would I still be a condescending wanker? Or does silence preclude wankerness? I just want to be clear on this.'

Five months into our marriage, standing in the car park of a sprawling out-of-town supermarket, I was overcome with frustration so jagged that I was bordering on despair. The details of the row are sketchy now but I do recall the glowering build-up over several days, the sense of isolation, the feeling that nothing I was saying was getting through to my new husband; and worse, that he did not understand me, nor I him; that we were stuck with each other and this was disastrous. I remember shouting, 'I never thought marriage would be like this!' and Mark replying calmly, 'What exactly did you think it would be like?'

Now, I can see we were simply getting to know each other – testing the limits of marriage, and realizing them, too. But there was no one to ask, 'Is this OK?' and my subterranean fears took some time to dispel. Before we married, it was possible for us to dodge the parts of one another we considered difficult. Permanently united, Mark found me less tender than expected – less than I had perhaps led him to believe I would be, once hitched. Close up, his personal crusades were as wearing as they were courageous. We worked effectively alongside each other but if, under duress, either of us sought consolation, comfort was scarcer than we had imagined; and whilst I had been a keen bride, I was an equivocal early wife. My better nature was pending, suppressed by concern that in our haste to be together Mark and I had sacrificed the security of knowing a bit more about what, precisely, we were getting into. It was almost as if I believed that by arguing as thoroughly as we did, and laying the foundations of all our fundamental disagreements, we might insure ourselves against later surprises.

What we failed to consider, however, was the importance of the context in which we were starting out. It did not cross our minds that whilst it might be recklessly satisfying to scream with frustration at your husband in a sleepy Mediterranean side street or to stride purposefully away from your wife into a crowded fish market, life in a small house in England would force us to scale down the expression of our conflicts. Indeed, married life at home did exactly that: it brought each of us into closer proximity and sharper focus, and for a good while after we returned from our travels, we both felt exposed. We found what so many people do, that despite the freedom conferred by a frank and enthusiastic union, sometimes there is not a lot of room for two people to manoeuvre in the tight space of marriage, and adjustment did not come easily to either of us.

It probably didn't help that wandering and caprice had featured so prominently in our previous lives. I had travelled and Mark, too, had disappeared, to paint in wild, open spaces; spaces which placed him exactly where he liked to be, uncontained by geography, four walls and even the most irregular of social arrangements. Before we met, he was evidently a man with whom it was burdensome to make plans and upon whom it was almost impossible to rely, ducking and diving in and out of numerous lives, leaving nothing substantive behind. However, he was in his mid-thirties by the time we got together and by then, returning home to a fax machine with its dangling pennant of fretful and cavilling messages had grown tiresome: a pleasingly productive week spent painting beneath a flapping tarpaulin was never enhanced by the admonition of women, assorted.

Mark installed me fast and now that he was flush with

love for just one person, the relief of monogamy was profound: for one thing, it meant that a homecoming was just that, and it made him happy. As for the fax machine itself, the long-time barometer of fidelity that was stationed in the open-plan living area of the Oxford flat (a rather risky location, I always thought), Mark announced with some considerable pride during the early days of his relationship with me that it had never been so quiet. Sure enough, not long afterwards the machine began to grind and whine, eventually discharging on a shaving of sleek, thin paper the indictment: '*It didn't take you long to move on, you bastard.*' 'That'd be Caroline,' said Mark, when I handed it to him. 'At least it's short.'

So, while it's hardly as if Mark deserves a medal for settling down, I do understand what an effort he had to make to be what he became, once married: a successful and audacious painter with friends and a wife; a well-appointed man lacking nothing visible. I see what a relief it must have been for him to feel that he could drop his guard. Now, there was someone else to do the things he found most exhausting, like deal with other people. Now, he could come and go as he pleased, knowing he had a safe haven to which he could return; and by coming and going, I don't mean buggering off in his Land Rover to paint for hours, I mean hitting the road for days on end, which was all very well when we were just a couple, for I would often go as well, walking happily along cliff paths or climbing hills to take photographs whilst my husband worked, but when the twins were born joint trips of this kind were untenable. Even when, instead of cooking our supper on a camping stove and sleeping under the raised canopy on top of the Land Rover, Mark and I booked into family-friendly B&Bs, with our baby paraphernalia and two self-assembly cots, it just didn't work any more.

It's the story of many couples, I know that, but when the children were born things changed between us. There was the delirious joy, the immediate shock of being deposed and then the long, slow burn of disturbance and alteration. Mark and I established a routine over time, its shape governed entirely by the needs of our twins and radically different from anything we had imagined. Sleep was pitted with cries and demands. Awake, the surface of our life felt immediately agitated and anything beneath the surface too heavily overlaid with exhaustion to produce any kind of fine sensation. Enlightened and debilitated by our charges our devotion to the twins was boundless but there was an awful lot of bickering, too. Almost all of it was procedural and almost all of it dull; heated at times but dreary nonetheless.

Communication between us had to change. Now,

shorthand was necessary because we were exhausted; because one of the girls was crying; because I was depleted from feeding two babies around the clock; because there was always, always something that needed doing. Mark's life altered too but as he never heard the babies' shrill entreaties he was never roused from deep sleep. He did a lot to help me but I became irritated by his inability to share the way in which my world had changed. 'You're knackered,' he'd say. 'It makes sense.' But that was not it. Now, we were divided further, by the crying of infants that punctuated my days and sabotaged my nights yet made no direct impression on his.

It bent us out of shape – I'd say permanently. A lot of demands upon Mark from our babies came indirectly, via me, which meant that during early motherhood my already significant role as broker and intermediary increased. More demonstrably than ever before, I felt myself an agent of exigency and exchange, as well as a petitioner for my husband's attention. Mark, in turn, would argue that he felt at a further disadvantage. He described himself as being unremittingly on call when he was working at home but without any terms having been properly agreed in the first place. In fact, it wasn't long before he took to appearing in the house with paint-brushes still in hand – a brand new form of defence against being inveigled into unwelcome tasks. In so doing, he made a kind of absurd tableau of the artist at work, standing poised and tense in the doorway of a kitchen littered with baby blankets and mugs of tepid, half-drunk tea. He muttered and sighed. I railed. Our friends said it was the same for them, too.

It wasn't, though.

Mark never wanted children. I knew this before we married but I didn't really believe him; or rather, I chose to ignore him. What I did believe was that because my desire to reproduce was in line with natural order and driven by biological imperative, it was more important than my husband's resistance to it. When he told me he thought himself unsuited to parenthood I told him that was rubbish. When he explained that he didn't trust either himself or the family unit, I said, 'Me neither,' knowing that to be the very reason I wanted to create some individuals I could love unconditionally who might also love me back without reserve – for I had things to make up for. And actually, while it is true I had little faith in the family unit *per se*, I did trust myself, just as long as I looked forward to what I believed a family might be, and not backwards at my childhood.

It took nearly a decade for Mark finally to capitulate. When I gave birth to twins, it was a double whammy of epic proportions. I fell in love with an extravagance unmatched by anything I had felt before. I was sated and whole, for the first time in my life. Mark, however, was suddenly a man with two daughters no longer than his

146

forearm whose safety and succour depended upon him as well as me. He was elated, of course, but the more that people told him what an amazing father he would be, the more he shrank from their compliments, convinced that he lacked the essential protective responses necessary for safeguarding his young. His insecurities peaked. Only much later did he admit to me that from the moment he observed the twins' first cries piercing the consciousness and soul of their mother, he felt, as never before, separated from me as if by a glass wall. Mark's involuntary response to the velocious clout of parenthood was the pain of a man now less of a participant, and more of an observer, in his own life.

Yet despite all that, our daughters could not have been gifted a closer, more attentive father. Infants learn to talk partly by lip-reading and they thrive on close visual attention. In their first year, Mark mouthed and smiled and crooned at our daughters: he watched them and held their gaze and with their soft, round heads cradled in his large palms, their legs kicking gently upwards in his lap, Mel and Miranda lay rapt as he chatted to them, eye to eye, eye to mouth. It was Mark who detected Mel's first word. Bent over her one day, his dark curls brushing her forehead, he called me over to verify her delighted repetition of a sound, as her small, wet tongue found a consonant to click rhythmically into the roof of her mouth.

'Listen, she's saying, "Ta Ta Ta"!'

'Yes! She is!'

'Or, is it, "Da Da Da"? What does it sound like to you?'

'Impossible to tell the difference. Oh, Mark, isn't she amazing?'

Mel gazed up at us, her eyes ablaze, thrilled with what she could do. 'Ta!' she said, and we squealed with delight. 'Ta! Ta!' As if to celebrate her multiplicity of skills, she lifted one foot and put it into her mouth.

'Oh, Mel-belle,' Mark sighed, kissing her toes. 'You clever girl. But you must never learn to speak from Daddy.'

'Darling! Don't say that!'

'But they mustn't. They'll sound wrong.'

'Don't be ridiculous. Of course they won't.'

'But you must be the one, Luce,' he said. He stroked Mel's left eyebrow and I felt faint with love for him and our children – for the family life we had created together. 'I mean it,' he repeated, 'You must be the one.'

If the twins exacerbated Mark's fear of being ill-equipped to cope with an amplified new world when he had worked so hard to come to terms with the one he knew already, it is unsurprising, looking back, that he felt the need to compensate. Newly fortified by self-doubt, he took on commission after commission. He disappeared for days on end for portrait sittings; longer still for landscapes. He took his car and stayed away.

In the first four years of our daughters' lives Mark produced enough paintings for separate exhibitions in London and Paris – for which he was praised to the high heavens. This generated more work, and at last, a little bit more money: we paid off our overdraft and for someone else to repoint the house's sodden west wall. Yet I calculated that in those four years, Mark was away from home for nearly a full two; and if you discount the hours he was asleep or working in the barn, his time spent with his wife and daughters was negligible. He hadn't wanted a family and his need to support us all justified not only his productivity but his absences. Whilst for me, family life was day-to-day fare, for Mark it was a rare departure from work. When he was properly at home with us all, I would hand over the children like batons in a relay race and he would take off, generated by an excess of energy garnered from the world outside. He was as invigorated, cheerful and confident as I was the opposite.

In the end, Mark agreed to having children because he did not expect me to miss out on them on his account. He made it clear, however, that they would always be his gift to me, and I was so relieved it didn't occur to me that indebtedness might harm us. It is true what people say, that nothing prepares you for parenthood, and it changes you in ways you cannot imagine. But what is also true for us is that even though Mark loves our daughters more than life itself, he still believes me to be ultimately responsible for the position he is in and for the strain he feels. 'It was your call,' he says, when we argue. 'I never asked for this.'

Di shoves aside a messy hillock of pillowcases and men's shirts topped with a crumpled *Trees of Britain* tea towel, leans across her kitchen table, and holds out her hand.

I turn my phone screen towards her as though I am presenting ID to an official.

'Oh, mate.' She stares at the photo of Angus. 'Why didn't you tell me sooner? I wish you had.'

'I thought you'd hate me.'

'How could you think that?'

'Because I hate me.'

'That's crazy. Oh, man.'

Tension that has been building up for weeks, months, it feels like a lifetime, begins to release; the guilt and confusion that never really abates. I picture Mark, stiff and subdued, and Angus, unfettered, and I burst into tears.

'Hey –' Di reaches into the ironing pile, pulls out a rumpled man's handkerchief – her husband Dave's – and offers it to me. I wipe my eyes, leaving smears of mascara across the white cotton.

'Now, look what I've done.'

'It'll wash out,' she soothes. She strokes my hand: a mother wanting a child to feel better.

I feel a fool. There are myriad ways in which a love affair is infantilizing and crying in someone else's kitchen is just one of them.

'How long?'

'Six months.'

'Oh, my friend. Bloody hell.'

Two summers earlier, when Di found herself exchanging emoji-heavy texts with a married colleague after hours, it was my kitchen table that served as a confessional. She says, 'You of all people should know you can tell me anything.'

'Telling you makes it real.'

'It's already real.'

'I still love Mark. That's never changed.'

She says, 'Why would it?' and then, 'How is he, anyway?' and there it is, in Di's polite enquiry, all the evidence I have never actually needed – that my best friend does not like my husband.

'Toughing it out,' I reply. 'He hardly talks about it. We did a bit in the beginning – talk. Now, he won't.'

'Helpful.'

'It's tense. It's like being in a waiting room. He's a hero, sitting it out.'

'I wouldn't go that far.'

'He could have walked away. I'm such a mess.'

'You seem to forget that he just buggered off when your kids were little.'

'He was working!'

'He was running away, big-time. You were practically a single parent. And now you're angry.'

'Maybe.'

'Mate, wake up! He's an amazing guy but he's selfish.'

'He loves us!'

'That is so not the point.'

I bite my lip.

She says, 'This is the man who left you on your own with twins and postnatal depression for a millennium.'

'He had a lot of people banging on his door.'

'I don't give a flying fuck,' she says. 'He neglected you. Bloody men! What makes them think they can reproduce and then just carry on as if nothing has happened?'

'That's not entirely fair.'

'It is entirely fucking fair! Listen, I understand he doesn't know how else to be but it's not your job to teach him. Yes, he's this cool artist who's overcome so much, etcetera, etcetera. But he's also just a middle-aged bloke with a wife and kids that deserve some attention. He needs to get over himself. Being unusual is not an excuse for being a crap partner.'

'I guess.'

She says, 'Right. So it's not just you that has some

thinking to do. He has to step up. Though you could stop idolizing him. That would probably help.'

When the twins were about six months old I realized I was afraid of almost everything. It wasn't something I really understood until I drove to a builder's merchant's out of town to pick up a new tap for the sink in the barn and felt compelled to write myself lengthy directions before setting off. It was only eleven miles and I knew the way perfectly well but I had lost confidence. I had the twins in the back of the car in their car-seats and all the way there I was badly on edge. Twice, I negotiated a couple of roundabouts to be sure I had the correct exits. I dithered at junctions while people behind me hooted their horns and flashed their lights. Eventually, traumatized, I pulled over and sat in a parking spot with the ignition switched off until I realized that I was going nowhere and there was no point just sitting there. When I re-joined the traffic, I found it aggressive and alarming: a turquoise Transit van was on my tail and everyone drove fast and with purpose, blending effortlessly with one another. It was as if they were communicating in a language I no longer understood but in which I had once enjoyed the ease and confidence of fluency.

Mark kept asking me when I might want to go back to work.

'Of course, we'll need help with the girls,' he said.

He might just as well have offered to sell them, or leave them out for the goblins to steal. If I was going to do one damn thing well, it was be a mother. Besides which, work that once meant quite a bit to me seemed both daunting and colourless.

Mark told me I was not myself. When I said, 'What the fuck do you expect?' he replied, 'My point exactly. You're so tense all the time. You barely speak except to criticize. It's not like you.' I told him I wasn't like me any more: I was a mother to twin babies and I was knackered beyond belief. I said, 'I can't think. I can't listen to music. I can't remember anyone's name. I don't even know what day of the week it is.'

He said, 'Do you think you might be depressed? I mean, I do. I think you are – depressed, I mean. You never laugh. You're not eating properly.'

'I am.'

He said, 'Babe, you don't talk to me any more.'

I looked at my husband, in his jeans and checked shirt, leaning against the kitchen door-jamb, one hand in his pocket, the thumb of the other hand in a belt loop; his pelvis tilted very slightly forwards. I thought, What on earth does he think he is doing, standing there like that? I did want company and in truth, I wanted only Mark's, yet looking at him then, I had a perplexing desire to tell him simply to go away. Nursing Mel, and unable to relax into her blissful, milky somnolence for I knew that Miranda was next – she was whimpering beside us on a flocculent, cream blanket – I could not give my husband the attention he demanded, just as he demanded to know what was wrong with me.

'I am not depressed. I'm tired.'

'It's more than that.'

'How the hell would you know?'

'Luce,' Mark insisted, 'listen to yourself.'

He suggested getting some friends over for supper, he thought it might be nice. Didn't I want to see people?

'No.'

'But you're lonely.'

'I have the twins.'

'And me,' he said. 'You have me. We have each other.'

My GP is away and his colleagues are fully booked. I see the locum, who says I badly need more sleep: she is concerned I am on the verge of severe depression.

'Can your husband help?'

'Not in the daytime.'

'How about at night?'

'He's deaf.'

'How does that stop him helping?'

'I told you, he's deaf. He doesn't hear the babies. He doesn't wake up.'

'Do you think that's reasonable?'

On her swivel chair, she sits with her hands folded in her lap and her head slightly to one side, frowning slightly. Does she believe that people who are really listening sit that way? Has someone taught her that?

'Reason doesn't come into it.'

'Okay, I know that but—'

'Right. So only I can hear them and once I'm awake, I'm disturbed. It's not his fault. It's not ideal but being deaf is not ideal, with or without small babies, though some would argue otherwise on the latter point.'

The locum smiles weakly.

'It's not his fault,' I say. 'I mean, for heaven's sake. Poor guy.'

'Have you noticed,' she says after a long pause during which she continues to nod gently, 'that you are defending him when in fact you are the one in need of some support right now?'

'I'm not defending him,' I say, 'I'm describing the difficulty.'

'Okay,' she says, slowly, 'I understand.'

You do not.

'It must be tough,' she continues. 'Deafness is a disability that others can't easily see, yes? It must be challenging.'

I think, *Why don't you go to an audiology conference? Read something on the Internet. Ask someone else. Just leave me alone.*

She suggests I sleep during the day and let Mark take care of the babies: 'Your husband is at home, so he could do the afternoons, perhaps?'

I point out that he's working.

'But from home.'

I ask her whether she would say that of a father who works somewhere else, like in an office.

'Probably not,' she concedes. 'But he doesn't.'

'It's a common misconception,' I sigh, 'that people who work from home can do what they please. They can't, not if they're going to survive. Plus, he travels a lot. I'm often by myself.'

'Do you have friends nearby?'

'Why?'

'Anyone who can help out?'

'Not really, no.'

'All right, then. What about your mum?'

'My mother?'

Fresh from my travels, I would spread my photographs across the table, a feast for my mother to enjoy alongside my carefully chosen gifts of textiles or scented oils.

157

She was keen to discuss the incidence of malaria, cholera, typhoid and stillbirths.

I wanted to tell her that I had never seen a sky so vast or so blue; that the smells and sounds of places touched me as much as the light and colours I tried so painstakingly to capture.

Her response never varied: 'But what have you learned?'

Women in iridescent saris with stacks of gathered kindling on their heads and men squatting around a brazier, their taut-skinned calves coated with a layer of road dust that had turned their toes silvery grey. I said, 'Look, they're preparing pakoras.' Skinny dogs in the streets. Black seals stuck fast to beaches like giant garden slugs. Children en route to school in crested blazers, small day-packs on their backs: 'Mum, look at those neat plaits between their shoulders. You've never seen such beautiful kids.' She wanted to know about literacy rates. When I showed her some rusting merchant ships on the Namibian coast, and men emerging at the end of the working day from a breaker's yard on the edge of Swakopmund, she asked me what proportion of the country's GDP came from shipping. At that point, momentarily, I cracked; I told her that their stance had made me think of Wilfred Owen's broken soldiers, bent double, like beggars under sacks. She said, 'Maybe. The trouble with pictures alone is they tell one so very little.'

So, I pulled out my ace cards. I took with me, to every country I visited, a mini cassette recorder. I gathered the dawn cries of the muezzins and the distant screams of high-circling vultures in the hot lull of a Delhi afternoon. I caught the yaps of the nocturnal infant tea-sellers as they jostled on the station at Darjeeling – their throaty assertions of 'chai-i, chai-i' in concert with the low rumble and metallic strain of the braking, midnight trains. I said to my mother who loves music, 'Listen! This takes you right there!' I played to her a group of miniature whistling frogs chirruping in a rainforest; I explained how I had had to sit stock-still and silently at the foot of a baobab tree, in order to capture the wild harmonies. She told me she had read something recently, about the country's lax sustainability policies. I said, 'But did you like the frogs?' She said, 'I would not have known that's what they were, from the recording.'

To the locum I say, 'What about my mother?'

'Does she live nearby?'

'No. And even if she did.'

'Okay,' the locum says. 'I see.'

'Devon,' says Angus, tapping the newspaper lightly with his forefinger and sighing contentedly. 'Now, there's a gorgeous place. Love to go there with you, one day.'

He twists around on the sofa to reach for his cup of coffee. The *Travel* section of the newspaper slides from his lap and spills on to the Persian rug.

'Bother,' he says. 'Can you pass that back to me, please?'

I gather up the pages. Photographs of Cornish beaches; descriptions of a petulant TV chef's trip to Vietnam.

'Thanks.' He settles himself back into the cushions. 'Are you happy, my darling?'

'Very. I love being with you.'

'You're my sweetheart.'

He says this a lot. I think he likes the way it sounds. *You're my sweetheart.*

'And I love being with you, too,' he adds. 'I haven't felt this easy with anyone, ever.'

'Oh, darling. Me neither.'

'It's just so nice,' he exclaims, as if he is in receipt of an unexpected bequest, 'being with someone who doesn't pick a fight!'

'Did Gill pick fights with you?'

'Sure.'

'But what did you argue about if you didn't live together?'

'Not living together.'

'Who wanted what?'

'She wanted it, I didn't. And she wanted to live in a house.'

'God forbid!'

'My sentiments exactly.'

'What's she doing now?'

'She's happily married, to someone she likes much more than she liked me.'

'Good for her. What about your other girlfriends? Did they argue with you?'

'All the time. In my experience, women pick fights pretty easily. You don't.'

'Why would I fight with you?'

'I don't know but it's a jolly nice change.'

At home with Mark, all sorts of things trigger my irritation, and his, and increasingly these days we make little distinction between what is worth contesting and what best left undefended. In short, we are happy to bicker about trifles. We expect easy escalation, can accelerate from stand-off to siege in a matter of minutes, and although we rarely succumb to spite, we have become unafraid of any impact that routine exasperation and pettiness may have upon our alliance. In short, we have grown dangerously unapologetic. If married couples are indeed complacent, it is because we stop being fearful. More fool us.

With Angus, however, my behaviour tends always towards the concessionary rather than the disputatious. Time is always too short and to waste it on minor grievances would be foolhardy, so I am more forgiving, and kinder, in my handling of the differences between us than I have ever been with anyone. I feign indifference. I conceal. Subterfuge and restraint. I believe our relationship is too fragile to support the weight of hefty disagreement. Angus disagrees, but he doesn't know what it is like to live in the better-fortified edifice of sworn partnership. He doesn't understand why I will neither take him for granted nor take him on; it doesn't occur to him that we could, all too easily, turn our fervour to our mutual disadvantage. He says, 'But what are you so afraid of?' and I explain that the relationship is not conducive to more heat than we already generate. He says, 'Nutcase, I don't quite follow you,' and I tell him we can't afford to burn our boats. He is genuinely puzzled. 'Don't be daft,' he says. 'If something's wrong, you must tell me, always.' But I don't, ever.

It troubles me, though, this inclination of mine to sidestep anything difficult. Just because every minute counts almost as much as every hour, and a day lost to simmering and carping could mean the possible ruination of that fortnight's precious allotted moments, doesn't make it right. I may never have lied directly to Angus but I am deceiving him at a fundamental level into believing I am someone I am not. On a boat named for truth, and willingly more self-exposed than I have been with any man, I fail repeatedly to face my own questions or respond to his, about our relationship, or our future, or our lack of one. On a boat named for truth, I dissemble like a courtesan.

I console myself with caveats: at least my equivocation – I hesitate to call it insincerity – is confined only to Angus. To Mark, faithfully, I deliver the truth always, however abrupt the admission – and sometimes, it is brutal. ('Yes, I've already said so: I love him.') But I am permanently queasy. I have set myself far higher standards than in my marriage. With Angus, the sparks that might ignite a row between Mark and me are given no oxygen, and – from this distance I have put between myself and my husband – I can only wonder now what might have been; what might have happened had I behaved this way with Mark.

I was fascinated by Mark when I met him. There was something so intense about the man. He seemed intent upon taking everything that bit further than everyone else. Prone on sun-loungers during our first holiday together, a trip memorable for its capricious weather, we agreed that nothing compares to the sensation of one's naked body being gently caressed by a warm breeze; that there are few things quite so sensuous. Yet on that same holiday I noted how, for Mark, moderate pleasures were rarely sufficient. The warm breezes we enjoyed were not enough for him. He was drawn to extremes – to profound gratification and ungovernable environments. Whether browning until he was positively carbonized, or head down in gale-driven rain on an altitudinous hike, his body acute-angled in dispute with the wind, it was easy to see that if ever a man took the elements personally, it was Mark.

'Angry,' Jay remarked, once. 'Mark is angry.'

Jay is wrong. Mark isn't angry, Mark is on alert – and that's different. If his quarrel with life appears never to let up it's because there are always things to consider; things that produce difficulties, or demand extra effort, like being in rooms too dark in which to lip-read, or with people who turn sideways whilst they talk. There are fire alarms, smoke alarms, car alarms; public announcements on tannoy systems; television programmes without subtitles; the high-pitched whine of a failing machine; the kindly stranger trying to warn him of something from behind; or the driver yelling, 'You fuckin' deaf, or what?' Years ago, while still at university, Mark got stuck in a lift. Unable to tell whether he could be heard calling for help, he had no choice but to wait, hoping the building was not on fire. Being suspended in the dark between the fifth and sixth floors of an office block was a sobering reminder of his vulnerability. In that lift – the last one he ever got into unaccompanied – being profoundly deaf felt as potentially lethal as deep water to a non-swimmer, and in a world filled with these particular perils, hazards and intimidations it's no surprise that he grew watchful and slick, ahead of the game. Quite apart from which – he explained to me once – a bit of strife here and there is invigorating. When you don't have noise, you need a substitute. When you can't even hear yourself breathing, you need to remind yourself you are alive.

Thus, Mark was always the life and soul, right there at any party's beating heart. Women, he could have them if he wanted them. Their physical presence he adored but his ability successfully to seduce them had a huge side benefit: it was proof of his superiority in this ultimate of male contests, despite an invisible but sometimes obstructive disadvantage. As a result, he spared himself the need to take on other men directly. He was a winner, Mark, not just of public awards but of private endorsements – from all those women across the rooms in their short, black dresses. He might have been too scared to get in a lift but he always got the girl.

And yet, despite Mark's best efforts and a lifetime of experience of keeping the challenges of deafness at bay, dullards make it through at times:

'How do you drive?'

'Surely if you turned it up full volume, you'd hear something.'

'You lip-read? Can you tell what that bloke across the room is saying?'

'You can't be deaf, you don't sound it!'

'How do you and your wife communicate?'

'So why don't you just get one of those implants?'

'Deaf or blind?' (a bunch of friends once contemplated, around our kitchen table). 'Which would be worse?'

'No contest. Blind is definitely worse.'

'Absolutely. No way I'd opt for that.'

I mouthed the word 'opt' to Mark. He raised his eyes to heaven.

I have never known anyone opt for blind as the lesser of two evils, deafness always wins, but only once the assembled company has taken a short imaginary excursion across soundless terrain.

'I'd miss the blackbird singing in the morning.'

'And music. I'd die without music.'

Blackbirds first. Then music. Every time.

'I'm still breathing!' Mark chimed.

I glanced at him, thought of the numerous occasions on which he had asked me, 'What's it like? Does it sound lovely?' All those times when friends rocked with laughter at quick-fire remarks that moved like balls too fast for Mark to catch: 'What's the joke?' he'd enquire, *sotto voce*. If we were out, I couldn't let my mind wander during conversations in case Mark missed details and afterwards wanted to know what exactly had been said.

I couldn't say, 'Nothing much,' as nothing much is precisely what you miss when you are deaf. Nothing much is the hue and tone of voices, the non-sequiturs, the nuance of tiny colloquial diversions. It's the bond between you and others that relies upon everything that is not mere content or transaction and feeling included depends on it.

'Sorry, Mark. No offence.'

'None taken.'

'Whereas sightless,' the conversation rumbled on predictably, 'you'd have no independence whatever. You'd need someone around, or a dog at the very least.'

'Couldn't drive.'

'So limiting.'

'Couldn't read, except for the odd book in braille.'

'You'd have audiobooks, I guess.'

'Couldn't see your kids smiling at you. Or the moon – or stars.'

It's usually this way: music and the dawn chorus pitted against the faces of innocents and the bloody night sky.

'You're so right,' Mark replied. 'Deafness is a breeze, by comparison.'

'Pal, I'm sure it's not.'

'No, it is; I'm serious. How can I mourn the beauty of birdsong when its sound – were it suddenly made known to me – might not be the thing I thought I had missed all that time? I have no way of summoning up even the faintest aural idea of what it is. Sound is like a vacuum to me, a nothing. I can't miss something that for me doesn't even exist.'

And so, conclusions were drawn that Mark is better off than most and everyone else far luckier than they generally recognize.

'We take so much for granted,' went the refrain.

Afterwards, Mark said, 'Don't you just love other people.'

'They're not thinking, babe. That's all.'

'You're not kidding. Fucking birdsong. There are a thousand other considerations.'

'I know.'

'Bastards,' Mark snarled.

'They forget, babe. It's because you're so adroit.'

But Mark's arms were in a circle on the table, his head upon them: he resembled a child slumped across homework that has defeated him. I put a mug down beside him, touched his shoulder. He looked up.

'Coffee.'

He shut his eyes and put his head back on his arms.

The few who understand there is nothing to recommend one life sentence over another tend not to get into conversations about deafness with Mark. Those others who do (sometimes because they are curious and sometimes because they want to reassure themselves about their own insufficiencies, and sometimes – to be fair –

because they have no idea how sorely he minds) like to tell him, 'At least you can do stuff if you're deaf. At least you can live a normal life. I mean, you're just brilliant, Mark. You're amazing. Look at everything you've done. Look at what you've achieved. Look at you.'

'Look at me,' Angus sighs.

He is peering in the bathroom mirror. Briefly, he reminds me of my father, inspecting something substandard over his glasses.

He says, 'I'm going greyer.'

'What?'

'Am I going greyer?'

'Yes.'

'Really?' He moves closer to the mirror. 'No!'

'Yes. In places, anyway. Those streaks at the sides.'

'Well, bugger this for a lark.' He pulls at the thick strands of hair at his temples, turning his head from side to side. 'Are you sure? Since when has this happened?'

'Since I've known you.'

'That's about ten minutes.'

'Don't be silly. But it was definitely a bit darker at the sides when we met. What's the problem? It's sexy. You look like a badger.'

'I don't want to look like a sodding badger!'

'Badgers are cool. Did you know they can unfurl hedgehogs?'

'Unfurl? What, like a parliamentary scroll? Do they eat them?'

'Yes, sometimes. They eat lots of small mammals. Mainly grubs and earthworms, though.'

'Blimey, the things you know.'

Angus peers more closely into the mirror, running his fingers slowly through the hair above his right temple. He wrinkles his nose.

'Stop preening. You're gorgeous.'

'I'm not. I'm old. I'm falling apart.'

He turns and looks at himself sideways on; he sucks his stomach in, pats it; sighs.

'I don't know what you see in me.'

'Your self-pity.'

'Hey!'

'Well, stop whining. I can get that at home, from my children.'

He looks at me. 'My godfathers,' he says. 'Tough talk.'

'Well, you're being ridiculous. You're only sixty, for God's sake. And I love you to bits, I think you're amazing. I'm here, aren't I?'

'You won't always be.'

'I will.'

'You won't.'

'Why do you say these things?'

'Because it's true. Quite apart from everything else, you will eventually find me too old. You won't want to come and look after me when I'm infirm, and who could blame you.'

If Angus knew how much I love his splendid, impressive face. If he had any idea just how beguilingly sexy I find all the evidence of a once-perfect frame in a body that has begun to creak a little and bend very slightly into itself. His skin is so soft and such a beautiful colour and it puckers a bit under my fingers. What is it that fascinates me so? I wish I knew. Is it the coexistence of strength and susceptibility? As for Angus's seniority, it feels like a sanctuary to me. He doesn't know that life without him seems impossible now, and he has no idea how hard I work to pretend I think otherwise.

I say, 'You will never be too old. You will always be my love.'

He puts his arms around me and treads on my toes. We are barefoot and the gesture is careful and deliberate. He places the ball of his foot across the top of mine and presses down firmly. I am shocked, for Mark does this, too, in almost exactly the same way, and I pull back slightly, as I never have and never do when Angus rolls towards me in bed and lifts me – his strong, flat hands in the small of my back – to position me exactly where he wants me, and where I too want to be.

I pull my feet out from under his. It is absurd that I find

it harder to accept his bare toes upon mine than his entire naked body, but I do. This is something that previously belonged only to me and Mark. 'Penguins' we called it, because we believed – possibly mistakenly, now I think about it – that Emperor penguins stand on each other's toes, and this we took as evidence of affection between these patient, portly birds; something uniting that also keeps the chill at bay. 'Penguins' became another element to keep us warm.

Where the shock lies: realizing how much and how little we share with another person that is unique. The combined history, the banter, a whole union's shorthand with which you understand that this is the marriage you are in, to that person and no other: what details of this fusion can we never expect to find with another person, in another relationship? What strange synthesis – that is already too extensive to recount and too abstruse or explain – belongs only to us? What sequestered familiarities? 'Penguins'? Not any more, it seems. Even they have negotiated with surprising ease the uncertain crossing from marriage to new romantic terrain.

I look down. My toenails are fuchsia pink, freshly polished. I am wearing a pair of rock-climbing trousers, in which I have scaled no rocks, and a checked shirt made from thick, brushed cotton that I bought years earlier in Canada: it is a man's shirt, small, part of what

Jay once termed my 'no-bullshit wardrobe'. It was a compliment, coming from Jay, but not everyone would see it that way. Angus has never seen this shirt on me before. In it, I fancy I look ready for anything: log-piling, chainsawing, digging ditches. In this shirt, occasionally, I imagine myself the wife of a Newfoundland fisherman. My hair is in a ponytail. The fisherman tweaks it as he walks past me, swinging a large diesel-stained oilskin bag on to a worn kitchen table and hanging the keys to his pickup on a hook in the wall.

Had I married Rich that is what I might have been, though Rich has probably given up fishing by now. He always believed we should leave the ocean well alone even before cod stocks hit an all-time low and the Canadian government closed so many of the fisheries. I wonder how he is these days. I think perhaps I will email him and find out. Funnily enough, Rich's feet loomed pretty large in our relationship. Except when there was ice or snow on the ground he would walk almost anywhere without shoes. His soles were filthy and the skin on his heels horny. Come to think of it, he was never quite clean enough for my liking but his ocean-salted, golden hair I loved, and the faint sweet smell of his hard, nut-brown chest.

I think back to the previous night, to where my feet were then; on *Verity*'s hazardous foredeck, glazed with rime, then padding around on her sanded floorboards while Angus cooked. As darkness fell, I perched them on the edge of the oval bath, my ankles crossed and my toes brushing Angus's left ear as we chatted until the water grew tepid and filmy: later, my heels jammed into his calves.

He takes my face in his hands.

'Imagine if we were married.'

That means unimagining everything I have.

He says, 'Okay, never mind. But please don't frown at me. A man can dream.'

A man with a woman can dream, and he should. But Angus and I are unable to plan anything, and dreaming is pointless, so we are denied one of the most fortifying elements of togetherness – restricted instead to shuffling pictures on the wall, chucking out chipped mugs and buying new bed linen in a role play of domestic re-arrangement. One afternoon, we move the sofa to another spot as if to underline our capacity to make changes against all odds, but it looks absurd and temporary; it was much better where it was in the first place. We put it back, to the spot where Angus originally parked it years earlier, by himself.

He says, 'Damn. I was really hoping for a change. Let's go out.'

So we hunt for a new kettle in John Lewis. I wait while Angus talks to an assistant about the model he wants that is not on display. The assistant needs to ask his supervisor. I get bored.

I say I'll see Angus in ten. I roam around, uninterested in Kitchens and nauseated by Perfumes. I take the escalator up one floor where, like a child emerging from the stuffiness of a wardrobe into a glittering fairy-tale winter, I am transported via Menswear to Lighting, before arriving in Bathrooms, where I find relief, at last, amongst synchronized displays of cream and white towels. And although it is months from Christmas and nowhere near Mark's birthday, I am overcome quite suddenly with the desire to buy my husband a thick-piled, shop-soft, dove-grey bathrobe. It is hanging right in front of me, in a row of other identical bathrobes: some are coffee-coloured, others white, but I want dove-grey. I know that once washed it will never feel quite the same again but the word 'dove' has made me feel calm, soft and airy – and I want that feeling to last. I want to feel dove-like. Even more, I want a dove-like husband. I picture Mark in the robe in our kitchen, coffee mug in hand, barefoot.

My phone pings.

'Nutcase, where are you?'

'In Bathrooms.'

Through a small square arch, I spy bottles of gold- and

silver-coloured liquids laid out along large white cubes. Maybe I should buy Mark aftershave instead. I can't leave empty-handed.

Angus appears from behind me.

'There you are!' He peers over my shoulder and into the bag: 'Ooh. Someone's bought herself a new bathrobe!'

'It's not for me.'

'No?'

'No.' I smile, embarrassed.

'You total sweetheart!' He grins. 'Am I allowed to put it on as soon as we get home?'

'Okay,' I say. 'Of course.'

Angus doesn't want to put any pressure on me but he does want to know whether I think things will ever be different for us, and if so, when.

He also wants to know at what point we might spend longer together. He says he understands my commitments but I know for a fact that he cannot begin to picture the reality: Mel and Miranda in bed with me on a Sunday morning, or all of us trailing round in our T-shirts and pyjama trousers, open books face down on the kitchen table beside cups of cold, greying tea, and the girls' bowls, cereal stuck like grouting to their sides, abandoned on the carpet by the television. Once, I tell Angus that on

Sunday mornings I make scrambled eggs for the girls – by which I really mean all four of us, but I don't want to say that. Angus knows this and says he would like creamy scrambled eggs on Sundays, too. He is going to hold me to it.

And so, because I do not want to try his patience too much, I am sitting with my phone and looking at my diary and going half-crazy with the seeming impossibility of the logistics, thinking, *I can't do that Saturday: Mark has a workshop in Bristol. Sunday is impossible: I promised to take the children swimming.*

I look out of the window. It is beautiful here today. Early summer. The sun is still up and the light forgiving. More time with Angus. Music, conversation, and lovely things to eat. The warmth of his skin down the length of my body. Best of all, his easy mood: a man that smiles when he sees me; always.

Mark could take the kids swimming by himself, I suppose.

I look at my diary again. Next weekend is impossible, and the weekend after that, and the one after that. Little things, commitments here and there, act as impediments that are not as great as my reluctance to upset my family's routine but are impediments nonetheless.

'*If any of you know cause, or just impediment, why these two persons should not be joined together in holy Matrimony, ye are to declare it.*'

You can hold your breath on your wedding day and breathe a sigh of relief at the silence that follows the question, yet sooner or later – when it comes to impediments declared and undeclared – you will find that marriage is full of them. Margie used to mutter, 'You can't get a quart into a pint pot.' I never understood what it meant at the time because for me, imperial measurements came under the aegis of history, not maths, but I think of it now as I wonder how I can divvy up my time so that I may fit the two lives that I have and the two men that I care about, into one – I know what Di would say if she were to finish that sentence; she'd say, 'Woman,' and I would say, 'No, Di, bugger off, it's not like that.'

Indeed, I do say precisely those words to her, at some point: 'It's not like that, Di. It's not the way it looks.'

But that's because I can't admit to Di how these days I reject Mark; that I cleave to my side of the bed and flinch when his foot brushes mine. I can't tell her that when I see my husband naked I look away as instinctively as if from a stranger; that the sight of him engenders feelings of such violent opposition I feel sick with guilt. I know it is in my expression sometimes, the visible rebound from what I once found lovely. Mark catches me not looking at him and I find it so hard to accept the pain it causes us both that I say to myself, even at those moments, 'But it's not like that. It's not the way it looks.'

'Darling, arrival time? xox'
'About 8. xox'
'How hungry? xox'
'Very! xox'
'Then I shall feed you until you are replete . . . xox'
If anyone were to read some of our texts, they might think it is exactly the way it looks.

He doesn't mean just a couple of days, he means an actual holiday.
'Do you fancy a few days in Devon?'
'A few days? Darling, are you crazy?'
'Of course, you can't.'
'I'm so sorry.'
'It's okay. I thought I'd just ask.'
'It's always worth asking, hey?'
He says, 'You can't do anything long.'
'Not really.'
'Or at short notice.'
'Not easily.'
'I can't just whisk you off somewhere.'
'No.'
'You're not mine.'
I put my arms around him. There are things I can say to console, or things I can say that are truthful.

Angus sighs.

He says, 'I belong to you but you don't belong to me.'

The television offers distraction from the decadent insignificance of our woes. We watch a documentary about a soldier who lost the better part of three limbs in an explosion in Afghanistan. Afterwards, he had one arm left. He was courageous and determined and said you have to let go of anger. He used the word 'selfhood' a lot and insisted he was still himself, still Phil – or Pincher, as he was known to everyone who loved him. His girl-friend had stuck by him through the lot: the injury and devastation, the rehab, the new house with its bars and rails and modified shower, and a bed with remote-control settings. She had to do everything for Pincher now. With the zeal of a religious convert, she too talked about his wholeness; she said what a great dad he would be in time.

Afterwards, I lie awake, worrying for Pincher and his girlfriend, wondering how whole you can be with one arm and no legs? At what point do you cease to be you? And if – like a film run in reverse – your limbs, one by one, were miraculously replaced, when might you say, 'That's enough! I am myself again!'? You are what you contain and not what contains you, that's the current thinking, and it's the way that Pincher and his girlfriend survive: but is it true?

'I belong to you but you don't belong to me.'

What particular days of the week does a relationship need to have, in order for it to be fully functioning? Is a man short of Sundays to call his own with the woman he loves short of something essential? Or are Tuesdays and Wednesdays the deal-breakers, freighted with the satisfaction and tedium of weekday routine? 'Amputee' was the one word that Pincher avoided using. Yet if ordinariness is our aim and I can't plan even a week with Angus, then is our relationship incapacitated to the point of being untenable? After all, if a husband is a man who can count on his tomorrows, then presumably for a lover, the opposite is true.

I get out of bed and go upstairs. I sit on the piano stool and look across the river and envisage the field behind my home, its skyline enhanced by trees, not eclipsed by buildings. Home, where until I met Angus, I felt gratified and safe. Home, where these days, I miss Angus so badly that I daydream constantly of a different sanctuary altogether, its mood susceptible to the elements and its light inconstant – and containing below the waterline in a bed beneath a crazy horse, libidinous, delirious us.

The children are asleep across the back seat in a mess of old cushions and books. Some of the books have been damaged by travel: bent, or their pages stuck together by long-ago spilt milk. Mel is sucking her thumb. Peter Rabbit dangles precariously from her lap, upside down, long ears hanging down towards the floor: *abandoned*, I think, remembering an afternoon with my own head tilted back at much the same angle as Peter Rabbit's, over the edge of the bed on *Verity*. Miranda is slumped like a drunk in a railway carriage, her long legs hanging heavily, her head inclined towards Mel, her arm in Mel's lap. Her mouth has fallen open and she is snoring softly. Baby snores. But Miranda is not a baby. Miranda is six.

What will I tell these children when they are older? Will I be able to explain myself in a way that is not, to them, entirely unbecoming? I doubt it. There is probably no account I could give that would bear the weight of a stranger's scrutiny, so why should my daughters be any different? If anything, they might – embarrassed, perhaps pious, possibly horrified – consider me wanton and foolish. I will doubtless keep quiet. The alternative will be to tell them that I love their father deeply but I let him down, and even though such transgressions are common-place, I cannot give reasons for my own infringement that are beyond reproach. What about the vows I made before a community of believers in marriage, if not in God? For better, for worse. In sickness and in health. As long as ye both shall live.

What if my daughters want to follow suit? (And why should they not?)

With my body I thee honour.

Forsaking all other.

I will say nothing. I will not explain to the young women they will become that I rarely break my word; that I believe in promises and they should, too, because promises give you the freedom to love another person properly. I will not tell them that the possibilities of love are endless and that it may be cherished or suppressed but it can't easily be contained; that it can be as wilful as a genie escaped from a bottle – which is fine just so long as you have infinite capacity for its expansion. And I will save them from my supposition – that you may be gay or straight, irreligious or devout, left-wing or right-wing, black or white, amiable or disobliging, even downright horrible, but if you are a woman attached in some way to two men, you may find the comprehension of others a bit beyond reach.

So, I will not point out that infidelity is not necessarily about what we do but who we pretend we are not. I will not explain that to love more than one adult at a time is inconvenient at best and shattering at worst, but it is not a crime. I will not tell them that because lying is mean and cowardly, I did not lie to their father, nor to Angus. It would give me more moral purchase than I feel I deserve, to present verity as a noble choice, and dissension from the norm as brave: it would imply that living truthfully is always an act of courage, when it is not – or not invariably. It cannot be: context is all.

Unless one day they ask me, and they wish for an answer. If they do, I shall tell them only this: that the possibilities of love are legion and should know no shame; and that sometimes, we do things that we ourselves find hard to understand.

As we approach a set of traffic lights, Mark says, 'Does that man have any idea what you walk away from every time you see him? Does he? Because that should have been his starting point. He's a child. He's a child because he has no idea what it means to have one.'

I feel it incumbent upon myself to defend Angus, as at times I defend Mark against Angus's charges of marital indifference. When the next available opportunity presents itself, I say, 'That's a pathetic argument. You can't suggest that any man without children is therefore a child himself.'

'I'm not. I'm suggesting that Captain Truth himself is particularly juvenile.'

'Who?'

'Captain Truth, Commander of HMS *Verity*, on which he lies with my wife – no doubt in some nautical hammock.'

'Don't be so ridiculous.'

'A musical hammock, perhaps. Does it rock you to sleep to Brahms lullabies?'

'Stop it.'

'Well, he's a child.'

'You don't know him.'

'I know enough,' says Mark. 'Life is different for men like him. They have no one else to consider. They are loose in the real sense of the word because they are completely unattached.'

The lights change and Mark begins to pull away. I think, *No ties that bind*. For all his solidity, Angus is vulnerable to every passing breeze. I picture the stays on the boat, straining against their only contact with the land.

'If he were serious about his life,' Mark says, 'he'd set himself some standards in his choice of woman.'

'What, like you did?'

But Mark can't see what I am saying.

'You are not his wife,' he continues.

'He knows that.'

'Why does he set his sights so low?'

'Thanks a lot.'

'Can't he get someone available, his age?'

'Mark!' I lean into his peripheral vision. 'Slow down! This is a forty limit.'

'He must think so little of himself.'

I think, *Car journeys are when blood is spilt*.

I picture Angus practising the piano, hair swept back from his forehead, shoulders raised, pursuant, intent, seeking amongst the keys what he can find there, and there alone.

At the next set of traffic lights, Mark looks at me and I say, 'Actually, no. I think he avoids thinking too hard about anything to one side. He's just like you in that respect: he concentrates only on what is in front of him.'

'He's selfish.'

'He's focused.'

'Regardless.'

'He's full of regard.'

The lights turn amber.

'Yeah, for you, perhaps,' says Mark. 'For himself, certainly.' The green light signals the last word, for my husband. 'Does he have a clue what it is you walk away from, to see him?'

'Probably not,' I reply, when he slows at a roundabout.

'Does he care?'

'I don't think he thinks about it.'

'Why would he? He has you and that is enough for him.'

But Mark can't look at me, so I can't respond. I think of Angus, quieter than usual one afternoon, his mood portentous, staring glumly across the giant slab of river, polished silvery grey in the noon light of a windless day.

'What's the matter?' I ask him.

'Nothing.'

'Come on, Angus, what is it?'

'You love Mark more than you love me.'

I hate it when Angus does this.

'See?' he persists, when I fail to respond.

'I have never loved like this before.'

'That's not what I mean and you know it.'

'Angus, I love you completely.'

'Maybe,' he sighs, 'but the fact is, I do not have the exclusive attention of the person that I love and that is depressing.'

I watch a distant police boat darken momentarily in the shadow of Battersea Bridge. A day-cruiser is heading the other way, towards it. Even from here I can see tourists outside on deck. They will have photos of the Power Station nicely in the bag. The police boat bends away and out of sight, in a last metallic flash of blue.

He says, 'I don't expect you to change your life for me, you know that. I wouldn't ask you to.'

I tell him that if we had children, it would be the case also; that he would never be the one and only. He says I know perfectly well that's not what he means.

When Mark slows the car again, I tap his knee to get his attention and say, 'I am not enough for Angus.'

He says, 'Then, why the hell?'

Arriving at friends' homes after journeys like this, our appetites wrecked by a glut of bickering, we get out of the car, stretch, and say, 'How lovely to see you, too!' And always, I wonder if they can tell.

Angus is sick and I go to him. I tell Mark I'll be back the next day but Angus has a high fever. I stay two nights.

The weather is squally and the bedroom portholes decorated with the residue of angry spray. I minister and tend. The tide is high. The boat rocks. Water everywhere. Outside, river and rain. Inside, tea, hot-water bottles, soup; liquids with which I express my love for Angus and further cultivate his trust.

'You are so kind to me.' His voice is raspy. 'I don't deserve you.'

'I do it because I love you to bits,' I say, which is true.

'That's helpful, nutcase.' He coughs and splutters. 'God, I feel awful.'

'Anyway, it's nothing,' I say, which is not true. It is not nothing to leave your family with frozen stew while you spend your evening, and theirs, making Lemsip in London for someone else.

Moving around the bedroom, I pick up Angus's trousers from the floor where he has dropped them. They have collapsed like an accordion, with his pants and socks concertinaed inside them. They look like cartoon characters that have been run over by a car and squashed entirely flat. I met a woman once, from Makuyu, in Kenya. A party was given in our village, to celebrate the twinning of our local secondary school with the high school in Makuyu. The woman's husband was there as well, tall and impressive, dressed in long robes of cream and burnt umber in tie-dyed patterns. He ate sausages on sticks and slices of damp, floppy quiche whilst numbers of Englishwomen in chunky Peruvian sweaters questioned him earnestly. He stood at least a head and a half taller than most of them and with their autumn skin and hair they looked overcast, like greying spirits that might fade in his summery proximity. I don't recall what got us on to the subject but with very little English on her part and zero Swahili on mine, the man's wife and I managed comfortably to establish that despite the divisions of continents and cultures, both of our husbands dropped their pants into their trousers and their trousers on to their socks, and the whole lot on to the floor, when undressing for bed.

I fold Angus's trousers and put them on the chair in the corner of the room. They're brown cords, soft and faint at the knees. I run my thumb across the worn areas. I am overwhelmed by how much I love this man. His underpants and socks I drop into the laundry basket in the bathroom. On the floor beside the bed there is the *Arts and Books* section from last weekend's newspaper, discarded; on the bedside table, a tablet strip now empty of paracetamol, its sharp, white plastic bent up at one end; and a glass, cloudy with use, with a chalky smudge across its base where the last of the water it contained has evaporated.

I stop. Something isn't right. I shut my eyes, concentrate, open them again. In the half-light, I see two small faces. It is the twins in their cot-beds, watching me as I draw the curtains, raising their arms in unison to be held and kissed: 'Mummy, Mummy, me first! Me first!' They are three years old. Or rather, they were.

The boat groans and lists. It is never quite the same, always moving slightly, always bearing risks – of the ingress of water, or breakages; subject to the vicissitudes of weather and tides.

From the bed, Angus says, 'God, this storm's severe. The piano's going to need tuning again after all this rock 'n' roll.'

'Not really the best thing for a piano, foundations made of water.'

'I know,' he says. 'I'm a chump. Tell me, how long do I have you, my darling?' From his easy tone, I can tell he is thinking another night.

'Three hours.'

'What?'

'The girls have an assembly tomorrow first thing, for parents.'

'I see.'

'I think we're all supposed to—'

He says it's fine, he doesn't need the details.

I ask if there's anything else I can do for him before I go.

He says there isn't.

Then he says, actually, he has a question he has been meaning to ask.

Mark says, 'France?!'

'Yes.'

'How long for?'

'A long weekend.'

'I see.'

I explain that I haven't agreed to it yet. I say, 'He has a recital, for one of his private clients; some Euro-Fatcat he's played for for years.'

Mark says he doesn't need the details.

'Obviously, I don't have to go. Nothing's fixed. I wanted to ask you.'

'What you do is your affair.'

When I ask him, is he being sarcastic? he says, 'What would be the point of that?'

* * *

In a sizeable chateau near the mountains, on Lake Annecy, Angus is playing Chopin and Schubert for sixteen people, with a bit of Scarlatti and Clementi on the side.

He explained his client to me before we came: a banker, Swiss, too rich and too flawless but – honestly – a nice guy nonetheless.

'A banker? Jesus, Angus.'

'I know. But *Verity*'s coming out of the water next summer. It'll pay for her hull to be stripped. And the grub is exceptional. Worth going for that alone.'

I imagined a Swiss-styled French chateau: ivory stone exterior, brocaded interior, everything quiet; furniture padded against the coarseness of life outside.

'We'll have to take a few formal clothes,' Angus warned.

'It's not cravat territory, is it?'

He said, 'I promise you, it'll be fun.'

I thought of Alan Bennett asking the actress Coral Browne, during a telephone conversation, the where-abouts of her husband (the actor Vincent Price). She replied that he was in America 'at the opening of something'. The opening of what? Alan Bennett enquired. A film? A museum? Coral Browne had no idea. 'Oh, you know Vinnie, darling,' she replied. 'He'd go to the opening of a manhole cover.'

I thought, *Call me Vinnie. I'd go anywhere, with Angus.*

The first few times Angus and I spent together we went

out on minor errands dressed up as jaunts and excursions: Tesco, the car wash, the post office and a key-cutting kiosk. They could have been the Royal Opera House for all I cared. I wanted only the proximity of shared experience with this man. In fact, the more prosaic the activity, the better, for the intimacy it implied. Our very first trip of this kind was to Homebase to buy some light bulbs. We might have been choosing an engagement ring, for the brightness it generated in us.

Now, hundreds of miles away, I am missing nothing more than the ordinary. Just a usual weekend: get up; do stuff; have lunch; do less; then supper, which bears us into the last segment of the day, with its bath-times and bedtime stories. But the ordinary is the constitution and I cannot help but feel that I have violated it. I see, too, that this is all it takes: a quick bolt on Eurostar and I am spirited away like a character in a fairy tale – the mother who is gone – and my children's routine is interrupted, if ever so carefully. I have left their favourite suppers, cooked ahead. I have bought special puddings, written a comprehensive list, reminded Mark of the babysitter's number. 'Remote control,' Mark calls it.

In the evenings, however, in the Swiss plutocrat's chateau, I wear silk dresses and my best jewellery, and Angus, in the nicest sense, wears me. He is visibly proud. Eating butter-soft slices of duck with potatoes shredded like matchsticks, my regret dissolves as I relax, knowing that my children are now sleeping and I am here to be entertained and perhaps also to entertain, in return. Our host is charming, his other guests are friendly and the conversation rich. I enjoy it all very much. Beside an Alpine lake streaked silver by a plump moon, and with Angus across the table, I am blissfully happy. Who wouldn't be?

Angus says, 'Oh, that went far too fast.'

I say, 'It really did.'

Mark says, 'We managed fine without Mummy, didn't we, girls.'

Arrivals and departures hang over us all, like clouds.

My sense of panic at waking in the wrong place increases manifestly. These days, when I am on *Verity*, I get up in the middle of the night. I look out over the river. Orange neon reflects back. *Overboard*, I think. I have fallen overboard and here I am, waiting for the tide to sweep me somewhere, to wash me up.

Angus sleeps. I have never known him anxious to the point of wakefulness. He shuts his eyes and drifts off, his feet and hands twitching like a dog giving chase in a dream until he comes to rest, his breathing a soft, steady snore. If I move, his grip around me tightens, unconsciously. I envy him. I cannot match his sense of where I belong.

Increasingly, when sleep arrives, dreams become nightmares. Everyday worries are swollen into menacing versions of themselves as I search for my daughters in stretches of black ocean. The light is gone, my panic increases, and only as the water dips and then rises into a thundering wall above me, do I comprehend that Mel and Miranda were never mine in the first place; that I am not a mother after all, and I am not married. Mark and our babies do not exist. I am a woman alone when once I was a woman, peopled. Alone, and soon to be overcome.

On waking, my body is tense, schooled for action that will not present itself here. Before, when I woke in Angus's arms, I would lie in his embrace, silently repeating to myself, *I am here, I am his, this is now.*

This is now. And now, awake, I listen to the family rising on the boat next door and curse the fact that Angus's neighbours are not all full-grown. The noises of children getting ready for school carry through air and water, and anxiety consumes me. Dearly, I wish those children were not there. I crave the sounds and feel of my own daughters, and the feeling intensifies each time I visit. Beneath the slatted, wooden ceiling I lie, thinking about all the reasons I have produced for myself to justify my presence here, and knowing they cannot convince me of anything but the truth: that as long as I wake up in *Verity*'s hold I am – as mothers go – at worst a fraud and at best a temporary absentee. In a few hours' time, I will be home again; but in the morning light of a city I do not love and in which I do not live I can defend myself to myself no longer.

There is a text from Mark, sent at 08.13. Mel needs her eye drops. Where are they? They are in my bag, is the answer – in the kitchen here. They shouldn't be but they are. Now, Mark will need to go to the chemist to buy some and then take them to school for her. It should be me doing that. It should. If I were away for work, it might be different, but I am not. I am soon to eat a croissant with Angus, on his roof.

At the end of the text, Mark has written: '*Missing you.*'

I am not hungry.

I get up. I see other children walking along the Embankment with their mothers and my homesickness and guilt translates to confusion. I don't know where the schools are, that they attend. Life in central London is a mystery to me. Where do normal things happen? The children I see here wear gingham-style dresses. The pattern is similar to the twins' uniform but in a different colour. Little kids, but not mine. I can't watch. I turn away, pace the short deck, observe the mud exposed by a low tide. It is humid and the sky is heavy. I shower and afterwards make coffee for Angus, wrapped in a towel. I try not to think about what is happening at home.

Next door, the littlest child and her mother are planting flowers in a tub. The littlest child is too small for school.

They look happy.

They have a tub on the roof of a boat.

Mel and Miranda and I have a whole flower bed. I can be a good mother gardening with her kids, for I have kids and a garden, and stuff to plant in it.

But for everything there is an equal and opposite reaction. I am here and my daughters are there, and I understand the equation. I am able to see how it should be. The answer is right in front of me.

I get dressed. I do not pull on one of Angus's jerseys over a pair of knickers: I did so in the profligate early stages, when the combination signified the kind of dissolution that I wanted to dwell in. I don't have the patience for that version of myself any more. I put on my own clothes, ready for a morning that I have disowned, and responsibilities from which I have already cast myself adrift. I am poised to chivvy and encourage other people into a full day but I am not where they are.

Re-entering the bedroom, I lean over the bed and touch Angus's cheek lightly. His face is rumpled, and slightly damp. The skin around his eyes, when he opens them, is creased. For once, he looks old. I don't care. Yet I am aware that he is at the unfamiliar end of life for me;

that the people I am missing are new, smooth-skinned, fresh.

'Hello, beautiful,' he murmurs. 'You're dressed already.'

'I made you some coffee.'

He reaches up for me, pulls my arm downwards so that the rest of me has to follow, for him to kiss. I am partially resistant, kneeling awkwardly beside the bed.

I can't see the Embankment from here but I know that by now the children outside will have disappeared and instead, there will be dog-walkers and runners, and people in suits and tight skirts walking purposefully along the riverside. Those who are talking and texting on their phones will far outnumber those who are not. School will have begun in London, in the suburbs, the countryside and elsewhere. The register is being called all over Britain.

'What time is it?'

'It's halfway through the morning for some people. Your neighbours are already planting flowers.'

'Meaning?'

'It's time to get up.'

'No cuddle?'

'No. You have to get up; you have practice to do.'

He yawns. His teeth are good. Good teeth, good hair, good skin. Good everything.

'Quite so, maestro.'

Good mood, too. How can a person be consistently so easygoing? He is always happy. Always. In the mornings, the first thing he does is beam at me. It's incendiary, the love that it begets. Bending over the twins' cots when they were babies, it was the same: their early-morning smiles set my heart on fire.

I stand up and Angus says, 'Shall I make us some pancakes?'

'Toast will do.'

'Hmm. Time was when you would have eaten pancakes all morning with me. Is something wrong?'

'No.'

'Good, because that reminds me: perhaps you'd like to have a go at pruning my pot plants.'

At home, last week, I pulled a lot of excess cow parsley – unruly, rampant, gorgeous, and stealing a march, as always, on the nettles. The earth was flinty and cool. On *Verity*, some terracotta water-cooling jars, large and Italianate, contain tobacco flowers and geraniums in Miracle-Gro potting compost.

He says, 'Obviously, you will know how to do it, nutcase, being a country girl and all that.'

It is such a reasonable request – for me to do this one small thing for Angus – but I am going to reject it. I am going to explain that I can't prune them because I'm useless with flowers but the truth is that I have no energy to tend anything else. Angus, I love. But his home, his environment, his carefully composed miniature garden – no. His babies I will never have. This boat we did not buy together. This city I would never choose. Why would I get involved with his geraniums?

I say, 'Honestly, I'm so bad with flowers.'

He says, 'Honestly? Honestly, sweetheart, you don't like it here, do you? London, I mean. Admit it. Deep down, you don't feel at home.'

And I think, *Never mind deep down: right here on top I don't feel at home.* Right here where my skin prickles and my eyes water and my hackles rise, and the breeze from the river feels foreign every time it catches me, right here on my surface I do not feel remotely at home.

'Seriously,' he says, 'do you think we will ever live together?'

I do not reply.

'Okay,' he says. 'Let's try a different question. When are you going to stop making excuses?'

'Flowers.'

Mark dumps four carrier bags of shopping on the kitchen table before passing me a bunch of white freesias.

'Wow.' I stare at them in my hand. 'Thank you. I don't think I deserve these.'

He crams six microwaveable cartons of lasagne and risotto into the freezer drawer, says, 'You're my wife. You get flowers.'

'Why have you bought all these ready-meals?'

'For me and the kids.'

'But why? It looks like you're stockpiling for a war.'

'Your analogy,' he says, running his hands through his hair. 'Not mine.'

I watch the curls slide and rearrange themselves around his face. It's something I always found pleasing, the way they do that.

'Luce,' he says. 'I want you to go away with him.'

Like a freezing wind blasting open a door not properly closed in the first place, his words tear into me.

'What?'

'Go away with him. Just bloody-well do it and be done with it. Go. Spend some proper time. I'll take the children to Cornwall with me.'

'What? No! We're all going together!'

'No. We're not. It's okay, I've talked to Jay and Lisa. I can share their au pair. We can manage perfectly well without you. They're up for it.'

'But I don't want that!'

'Well, it's kind of too bad, Luce. Because I'm damned if I know what you want, either. All I know is that I am sick of this. Don't argue. Please. I've decided.'

'But Mark!'

'It's fixed. Don't panic, we'll all come back. But then that's it. After that, I will do no more.'

My ears are ringing. I begin to shiver. The weeks ahead

will shrink to days, and then hours, and then minutes. Time will run out and I will no longer be able to avoid having to face the end of something.

Holes everywhere. The bastards have eaten through four of Mark's jerseys, and two of mine: they are beyond repair. I am up to my eyes in moth repellent, folding our wool stuff in zip-lock bags and thinking how my relationship with Angus has eaten away at the fabric of all our lives; how just like a moth-eaten garment, everything now is pockmarked by holes. Holes in my marriage, and holes in Angus's life, with me: holes in our appetites, our sleep, our self-respect, our sense of what is real. All our formerly unabridged lives are now divided, and what, before, were relatively smooth passages through the weeks and months have become a confusing and un-edifying mess. It makes little sense, to any of us. It probably looks insane.

I put the jerseys in a bag in the porch, ready to take out for recycling, and regretting in particular the loss of the pale pink one Mark bought for my birthday the year the twins were born.

Just inside the porch, standing on one leg, and so still it might be inanimate, is a bird. It is a sparrowhawk, not a rare bird but certainly uncommon and not one to choose proximity to humans. I have never seen one so close before. I approach it cautiously but it doesn't move; its head is downward but not quite tucked into its breast, as if it cannot muster the energy to get properly comfortable. I look into its nearest blank, onyx eye. Statue bird. I am not even sure it registers me.

I don't know what to do, so I ring the RSPB helpline: I tell the woman who answers that the bird is surely sick and I am worried it will die tonight. 'Leave it,' she advises. 'There's not a lot else you can do. It will almost certainly fly away.'

'It won't, I don't think. But thanks, anyway.'

I go outside again twice, the second time just before midnight, to see how the bird is getting on. It doesn't budge. As I lean in towards it, its tail feathers twitch very slightly and it defecates.

'Sorry, birdie,' I say, backing away. 'Sorry.'

I lie in bed, trying to picture Mark and the twins at Jay and Lisa's place in Cornwall. They'll go to the beach in the morning and eat cake at the cafe overlooking the bay. Lisa will be leaving in a couple of days, to run an obstetrics course at a hospital in Sierra Leone; the au pair will take over. Lisa's children, too, will briefly be motherless, but with good reason. The cause of her not infrequent absences is unimpeachable. Jay will want to know why it is that I am sleeping in London, with another man – if Mark tells him, that is. It will be difficult for him not to. I worry. I have put us all in a terrible position. The problem feels too intractable to be real.

The sky outside is starless and so black that I can only just make out the odd shape in the room. Since meeting Mark, I have begun to treasure the dark, in the way you can come afresh to cherish an old friendship long taken for granted. The blankness is consoling, a respite from busyness and confusion. We live a life of clarity and lustre, Mark and I. Our windows are clean, our walls white. Gloom and shadows make lip-reading hard, so everything we do is illuminated. Overhead lights are ablaze even on bright days. It was a bit of a shock when I first got together with Mark, adjusting to the glare. I have made the case for strategically placed low lamps but soft lighting only irritates him. I have never had a candlelit supper with my husband. We make love with the bedside light on, or we did. I was self-conscious the first few times that happened. I felt like a subject, lit – and once, when drowsy and full of wine, the thought crossed my mind that if I married this man I would be in the spotlight always, cast permanently in a strong supporting role in the silent movie of his life. 'Don't be daft,' he laughed, when I put it to him. 'You're my leading lady.'

I remember one of the first things I said to Angus: 'Turn off the light and keep talking. I want to be loved in the dark.'

When I open the front door, first thing in the morning,

I am hoping to see the bird gone. Rigid, it is lying on one side where it has fallen. There is a large, pooled mass of unnatural-looking white foam emanating from its mouth.

'Ohhh,' I say, recoiling involuntarily. 'Oh, poor you.'

I find some thick gardening gloves in the porch and gently lift the bird in both hands. Is it infected? Was it poisoned? I am repulsed, and ashamed of being so, by the small body that once contained life and does so no longer.

I place it out of sight around one side of the house. I can bury it later, before I leave. Right now, I must deal with its toxic spew. Running hot water and bleach into a bucket, I notice a large crack running vertically up the wall, in the corner of the room. I've seen it many times before but its significance has failed to register until now. Subsidence. Oh God. Now, my house is falling down.

I sigh. Everything feels sad.

Di says, 'Sorry I didn't call back last night. I was wondering which moron was trying to reach me in the middle of *Top Gear*.'

'This one. You know, you really are a bloke.'

'With very big tits. Where are you now?'

'On the train.'

'Have they left already?'

'Yesterday morning.'

'Does it feel weird?'

'I'm already missing the girls like hell. But Jay and Lisa's kids are like cousins to them, and Mark will get to paint his Cornish stuff.'

'And you're en route to a fortnight with Angus!'

There is a scuffle at the other end of the line, followed by a noisy clatter. 'Brian!' Di snaps, her voice muffled but clearly raised. 'No!'

'You okay?'

'Fine,' she says, more clearly now. 'Never get a Jack Russell.'

'It's not on my list.'

'Good, because you'd only have another aggravating chap to attend to, and you've presumably got enough of those already. Are you excited? You must be.'

'It's just a break, Di.'

Di sighs.

'I really hope this works out for you,' she says. 'You don't sound very okay.'

'I'm such a despicable person.'

'No, you're not! You haven't deceived anyone.'

'It only makes me not a liar. It doesn't make me a great wife, or a great mother, or a great anything else, for that matter. I'm beginning to think the truth is almost as damaging as deceit.'

'No way. Deceit is far worse.'

'Possibly, but if you're causing pain to people, the

difference that telling the truth makes is probably negligible. And in a way, being truthful has its own particular pitfalls. Bit by bit, you let yourself off your own hook by reminding yourself of your own fidelity – ha bloody ha – yet the fact is, you're still making a mess, regardless.'

'As in, you're off to rob a bank but as far as you're concerned, it's okay because you've told someone beforehand that's what you're going to do?'

'God. When you put it like that.'

Di says, 'Mate, listen. I'm not judging you. The truth is, I'm sitting here as married and bored and disappointed as the next woman, watching you do something I would do myself, if I had the guts. If I could be on a boat, away from Dave, having amazing love with a dreamy-looking musician, I'd be there like a shot.'

I tip the contents of my bag out on to the bed. 'Our bed', Angus calls it.

In amongst the jeans and jerseys are a few new things: lace and silk underwear, a short cotton skirt, a silk summer dress and a couple of decent blouses. Lipstick, mascara, rose-pink nail polish, and a bikini, in sailor stripes; French, and slippery with newness.

'Here I am,' I say. 'This is it. This is me.'

He gives me a set of keys, and with them a bunch of

flowers. He says, 'You mentioned once that you love freesias,' and, 'Now, you can come and go as you please.'

Later, I walk by myself to the nearest grocer. That way, I can return with milk and eggs, and say, 'Hello, sweetheart, I'm back.'

He says, 'Shall we take a look at the Impressionists exhibition?'

He says, 'Yippee! No more teaching and no more gigs until September!'

He says, 'The weather's looking fantastic for our trip.'

He says what people say when time is on their side.

There seem suddenly to be a lot of parties. Behind imposing white-stuccoed houses, in gardens saturated with roses, Angus introduces me to his friends.

They say, 'Where did you two meet, exactly?'

'How long have you known this old reprobate?'

'What is it you do?'

'And you live where?'

I take long, hard looks at the women. Angus is not eyeing up these musicians and agents and college administrators and gallery curators, but I am. They have eaten reasonably and exercised moderately for most of their lives. They have long-held interests and reservoirs of knowledge. Clear skin, attractive clothes, well-cut hair. There's evidence here and there of the odd procedure but for the most part they seem to have shunned plastic surgery, and if not, they have kept it subtle: for them, it seems, excess of anything but work is a vice. They are stylish, elegant and forceful. They have a fair number of marriages and divorces under their belts. They have clocked up achievements, reproduced well into the future, been lost along the way, and survived. They have, it seems, nothing left to lose, no deterrents in the pursuit of more.

We talk about children. Mine are the same age as their grandchildren, so our conversations have an adjacent quality. Angus is protective. He rests his chin on the top of my head. Some of these women pursued him in the past, or he them. A few say, 'My God, Angus, you do look loved-up!' or variations on the sentiment, in front of me. Most of them mean it kindly.

Driving back to *Verity*, I say, 'I can't recall seeing so many beautiful women in one place. What is it about women in their sixties? They're powerhouses.' Angus says, 'I've never really thought about it,' and I say, 'Well, you should. We all should. We might learn something. Maybe it's because they've reached an accommodation with life.'

Occasionally, I ask Angus what they mean to him, the

women he knew before me. But his previous relation-ships he recalls as he might a series of good meals eaten years earlier; with a pleasure that is abstract and hazy.

I think perhaps it is because he understands how easily the past may be obliterated by the present, that pasts of all kinds seem to have little meaning for Angus. I say, 'But didn't you ever want more?'

He says that just knowing someone was there was suffi-cient for him; he admits that anything more would have meant unnecessary clutter and effort. I say, 'What, you mean like reciprocity?' and he says, 'Well, I suppose so, nutcase, yes, though that doesn't sound very nice. Look, it's not like I've never cared about people – of course I have. But I've changed. You know that.'

'I'm quite relieved I never knew you before.'

'Thanks!'

'But you've spent your whole life avoiding anything accidental happening to you.'

He says, 'Until now.'

Now. When my clothes hang in his wardrobe. When in the bathroom – 'our bathroom', he calls it – my bottles of assorted fripperies on the tiled shelf outnumber his. When the key to *Verity* has a permanent home in the inside pocket of my bag, and attached to it is a keyring with a small blue-and-white painted wooden boat, roughly hewn, the grain visible through the thin paint; a gift from Angus. Written in his recently renewed passport is my mobile phone number. If, whilst playing in some overheated palazzo, he suffers a heart attack, mine is the number to call. Across time zones and continents he has the comfort of knowing I am his and that in absentia I may be summoned if need be. In sickness, if not in health, I belong to him on paper. In black and white it is official, with a government stamp.

'Look,' he says, grinning, indicating our clothes on the floor beside the bed, our mugs in the sink, my earrings in the bathroom. 'Anyone would think we were married.'

But real partnership thrives on tomorrows: we both know that. It depends on the steady assumption and accumulation of the future, not merely the co-mingling of items, and as time goes on, the difference my temporary presence makes to the two of us is not clear. Angus tells me he is scared for the first time in his life. It occurs to him that love may not be enough; that, at best, he might find himself waiting for some time – and for what, exactly? Isn't that what often happens in a situation like ours? He says the purpose of telling me is not to make me feel bad and he knows I have a life elsewhere, but our relationship has slowly bred in him the feeling of being in captivity.

I can't tell Angus that for the very reasons he feels imprisoned, I feel liberated. I have nothing to lose – at least, not right now, right here on this boat – because with him I have nothing ventured: no marriage, no children, no house, no money, and no future dependent on our joint protection of any of these. With this absence of investment comes the freedom I have never experienced: to love without intent. *I am his. He is mine. This is now.* There is nothing else.

I say, 'But Angus, you don't understand. I have never loved anyone like this before.'

'No one?'

'I think if you have marriage on your mind when you meet someone, it can get in the way of loving the person only for himself. If you're considering all along what kind of husband someone might make it can cloud the issue slightly. For women, anyway.'

'I am sure for men, too.'

I think of Mark before me and the twins, painting freely under his tarpaulin.

'Yes,' I say. 'For men, too.'

In the bath, the water is so high that if we move too suddenly it sloshes up and over the edge and on to the floor. Angus's hair is partially wet, slicked back from his forehead. Steam rises from the water's surface, its sheen sitting lightly on his skin. He looks so sculpted and commanding that I want to lick his face. I want to run my tongue along the line of his jaw and the slab of his cheek;

to luxuriate in its soapy heat and evening roughness. I want to make him wholly mine, with my mouth. I don't lick him. I stroke his thigh, slippery under the water, feel the muscles beneath his skin.

Verity shifts and creaks.

I say, 'Do you ever think it odd that when we are in the bath we are in water, under water, but never actually drowning?'

'Happy end of your birthday, my darling.'

The night-scent from the tobacco plants in their large pots is full-bodied and sweet. It's nearly bedtime and still hot – so hot that we have eaten every meal outside this week, on deck.

'Thank you, nutcase.'

I say, 'What a wonderful evening.'

He says, 'And what a wonderful day you've given me.'

'Here's to you.'

'Here's to us!' He sings, '"Will you still need me, will you still feed me, When I'm sixty-four . . ."'

'You're sixty-one.'

'I'm just covering my bases. Making sure you'll be here then.'

'Of course I will.'

He hands me a small box.

'What's this?'

'It's for you.'

'But it's your birthday, Angus, not mine.'

'I know but I've been wanting to give it to you. This seemed the perfect day.'

'Are you sure?'

'Just open it.'

His eyes are shining.

'Oh, my goodness; my darling.'

'Do you like it?'

'It's beautiful.'

'It was my mother's.'

I slip it on to the third finger of my right hand. Aquamarine.

'I'm overwhelmed.'

He smiles. 'It looks lovely on you.'

While Angus is brushing his teeth and I am tidying up, Di calls and says, 'Sorry if I'm interrupting anything. I just wanted to catch you before you go on holiday. It is tomorrow you leave, right?'

'Yeah.'

I tell her about Angus's birthday.

She says, 'His mum's ring! Wow!'

'I know.'

'You sound really happy.'

'I am.'

'What'd you give him?'

'A bodyboard, for taking on holiday. He's already had a new bathrobe.'

'Darling nutcase!' Angus had roared with laughter when he saw the board propped up against the fridge. 'What am I supposed to do with this?'

'It's for Devon, silly-billy. You said you'd never tried body-boarding. Now's your chance. I bought it from Amazon, it came two days ago; I had to hide it in your spare room. Anyway, you're such a Tigger at heart, it seemed perfect.'

'I'm an ancient Tigger.'

'It'll keep you young.'

'My darling girl, it'll be a shortcut to A&E. But I commend your good effort all the same.'

I also bought him a giant bottle of bubbles, to blow from the boat's prow towards the river, which he did, at breakfast-time. I baked him a cake shaped like the letter A, and placed mini sparklers in the chocolate icing. I gave him a pair of oven gloves printed with the words '*Too Hot to Handel*' and a small, soft corduroy lion with a wavy mane. Angus placed him, immediately and prominently, on a shelf in the kitchen. 'King of the Feasts', we named him.

In the hotel's best room, the one with the biggest balcony directly above the beach, he angles us in front of the mirror, his hands in my hair.

'Look at this beautiful view,' he says.

He picks up the envelope on the bed.
'What's this?' He looks suspicious.
'It's for you.'
'I can see that.'
'Open it.'
'What is it?'
'A poem.'
'"Wring Out My Clothes",' Angus reads. 'You sure it's not a form for hotel laundry?'
'It's a poem. By St Francis of Assisi.'
'Blimey, I didn't know he wrote poetry.'
'He was a man of many parts. Like you. Read it to me,' I say. 'Out loud. It's very short.'
Angus reads:
'"Such love does
the sky now pour,
that whenever I stand in a field,
I have to wring out the light
when I get
home."'
I say, 'This is how it is for me, being with you.'

* * *

The sea is not as blue today as it was yesterday, or the day before. It has a pale charcoal hue, except in places where the tide is breaking its surface into fidgety, silver curls. Close to the cliffs the waves are strong. I watch them for a while, hurling themselves against rock, unyielding.

I can see him on the beach, reading. He looks a very long way away. Only a few hours ago he was so close that I could see the flecks in his irises. He looks up briefly, locates me, waves. I wave back. 'Watch me,' I want to call out. 'Watch me!' But he doesn't. He watched me earlier.

The waves are more powerful than they were on the day we arrived. I hold on to Angus's board and I paddle hard but progress is slow. I keep getting knocked back. I think of the sea in France, early in my marriage, where there were no waves to speak of. It's a while since I've bodysurfed in swell this rough. I wonder if I've lost the knack. The morning sun is in my eyes. I look away from it, westwards, down the coastline. My babies are some-where there.

Jesus! All of a sudden, the light disappears. I have no idea which way is up, which way is the seabed, and where the sky has gone. I feel my neck rip, there's a fire in my shoulder, but I am too busy clawing at the water. I know I have been hurt, I know this for sure. I scrabble, trying to find footings, sand, something solid. What has happened I don't know. A wave I did not see coming.

The water has inhaled me and now, being rolled and pummelled as if I am something it took in error, something it does not want and is preparing for disposal, I am to be reduced and deformed. I can hear the tide, the swell of heavy water over tiny particles. I flail, hoping to hit something firm. There is only the insistent surge. I do not want to be swallowed. As a child, I would wake on occasion coiled at the bottom of my bed, humid and blind, panicked by the tight smother of blankets over my head, and like a swimmer in the deep end of a pool I would kick until I found the wall through the bedding, and propel myself upwards to air and space. The way was narrow but straightforward. Now, I do not know where I am. I fight. With one foot, I make contact with the seabed, but I lose it again, feel only the sharp abrasion of packed sand along my left hip.

As abruptly as I was overcome, I am expelled. I gulp for air, mouth full of salt, the taste repulsive. I hear my coughs, jagged and harsh. I am choking. Yet more water slams into my face, tearing at my skin: it's in my eyes, down my throat, up my nose; I can't see, I can't swallow, I can't breathe. I am being murdered. It feels like indifference, what the sea is doing. A revelation: *Violence can be entirely arbitrary*. My body is contorted, the sensation in my torso is of twisting ropes. Spikes of sun are in my eyes. A cloud turns too quickly on its axis. I wonder, fleetingly, *Where's the board?*

The smack of water on the right side of my head is so powerful I am knocked sideways once more. My ear explodes. I am held under, crushed by waves like a downpour of cement. I gasp but there is nothing. My insides are ablaze. Something pulls at my left arm – once, and then again. I understand this is terrible. *Nutcase, you can't breathe.*

There are people close by. Towels. Flasks of tea. A lot of legs, flip-flops and bare feet. A man is crouching, his hand on my arm, his swimming trunks stretched tight across his inner thighs, his calves hairy and taut. I can't see his face easily. A woman is leaning over me, strands of salty hair skimming my face as she talks to me in tones I use for my children. 'It's okay, babe,' she says, 'it's okay now.' I can't see her face, either. Blue bikini top, large breasts; nice ones, men will like her. People slightly further away – an outer circle, milling, chatting to each other. Their interest – piqued – keeps them nearby.

Angus.

'My darling,' he is saying. 'My darling.'

He is beside me. I can't lift my head or turn my neck to look at him. But I know his are the hands holding an unfamiliar-looking metal mug. He raises it to my lips.

'Sweetheart,' he says. 'Try to drink.'

I can't.

Someone says, 'Might be best to leave it. She's in shock.'

'Babe,' says the woman. Her voice is husky. A smoker, perhaps. She is crouching now, like the man with the taut trunks and calves. Silver bangles jostle for space on her wrists. 'We think you've dislocated your shoulder, yeah?'

I have? A croak at the back of my throat; a mild objection to the news.

'It's okay, honey,' she says. 'They'll sort it for you at the hospital, you're going to be fine. But we have to let them do it, yeah?' She strokes my wrist and I flinch. 'The pain's really bad?'

I try to nod but I can't do that, either.

The shivering won't stop.

The woman turns to someone standing behind her, enquires, 'Are they on their way?'

'Yes.'

'Oh, sweetheart,' says Angus. He asks, 'Does anyone have another rug?'

Pass the Parcel, where you take the layers off one by one. This is the other way around. They keep adding to me. I am a mound of fleecy blankets and someone's jacket. 'Mind her shoulder!' Angus kneels on all fours in front of me, stooping very low, his head bent so that I can see him. He looks like a child pretending to be an animal. He seems very worried. I am puzzled. His face has gone black

220

and white. There is no colour whatever. A treble buzz begins in my ears, expands to a screech.

'Lucy!'

'It's okay, mate.' I think someone is reassuring Angus. 'Pain does that.'

A different voice, a new one, 'What's happened?'

'She just fainted.'

'She's vomited.'

I can feel my cheek congealed against wet sand.

'She fainted?'

'It's the pain.'

'Shouldn't we sit her up again?'

Hands on me; damp. They try to move me.

'Lucy, do you think you're going to be sick again?'

My neck burns.

'No, stop!' someone says. 'Wait for them to get here.'

'Yes,' I hear the new person say, in a telephone voice. 'Yes. She's with her husband.'

In the ambulance, they give me gas and air. By the time we reach the hospital, the pain belongs somewhere else – possibly even to someone else. I think of a dog on an extending lead.

'It's like that,' I say. My voice sounds thin and remote.

'What's like what, darling?' Angus asks.

'A dog. Pain. It goes away from me.'

I can't keep my eyes open.

'Are you there?' I keep saying. 'You're still there, aren't you?'

'I'm right here. Don't try to talk.'

The A&E nurse is practised and swift. Once my shoulder is back in place, the relief is immediate.

She tells me that she will put my arm in a sling, and she tells Angus the way to the hospital pharmacy, where he can take the prescription for my painkillers. He says before he goes, 'Sweetie, do you want anything else?'

'I just want to go home.'

'Sinéad,' he turns to the nurse, 'I can't thank you enough. Can I get you a coffee?'

Sinéad says, 'I only drink whisky when I'm on duty.'

'Marvellous!' Angus replies. 'At last, a woman who speaks my language.'

When Angus is gone, she says, 'What a great husband.'

'He's not my husband.'

'Oh, sorry.'

'I am married,' I say, 'but not to him. He's my – my boyfriend, I suppose. I don't know how to put it, really. My husband knows.'

'No problem,' says Sinéad. 'Main thing is, you've got

someone to look after you.' She lifts my arm and places it in a diagonal across my chest, as if I am about to swear allegiance to something. She says. 'If you could just support your elbow there for a moment with your other hand.'

I wince. She asks me how much it is hurting on a scale of one to ten if ten was the pain before she put it back in.

'About six, as long as I don't move.'

'Okay, that's fine.'

'Yeah, for you, maybe.'

She giggles.

'Sorry if what I just said seems weird to you,' I say. I am embarrassed.

'I promise you, almost nothing seems weird to me.' She adjusts my arm slightly.

'Ow.'

'Sorry, pet.'

'I wouldn't want you to think that it's just some horrible, hidden thing. It isn't. It's nothing like that.'

I am talking too much.

Angus has asked me several times, 'Why do you care what people think?' And Mark has asserted, repeatedly, that when it comes to other people and their opinions, he doesn't give a damn either way.

But I do. I care because for all my don't-give-a-damn attitude, I do give a damn. I don't want to be a pariah. I love Angus, I do, but I have liked marriage, too. From the beginning, I have been grateful for its less refined points; its temperate climate and steady, repetitious nature. There is something to be said for the refuge of the commonplace. Yet I have been drawn always to the unfamiliar, to the kinds of people for whom strange, new lives must be lived. I wonder occasionally, *Should I have sought something more extreme?* Rich and Newfoundland were the closest I ever got: a man in a canoe, his hands salty-rough; the local women with their tram-lined skin and pocket knives, resilient. Cod hauls, high winds, and knowing there were bears in the hills. In bed in wild Canada, I would lie awake in thrall to the peculiar.

Sinéad says, 'I wouldn't think anything. Don't you worry.'

I ask her if she sees a lot of surfing injuries. She says, 'Is the Pope Catholic?'

'So, you're like that guy with the clipboard in *The Life of Brian*.'

'The crucifixion guy?'

'That's the one! "Crucifixion? First on the right. One cross each." Dislocation? First on the right. One sling each.'

She laughs. 'What is it with that film? My ex-boyfriend could quote every line. The tosser.'

'So can Angus. So can I, come to that. Maybe that tosser ex-boyfriend of yours is actually me in disguise.'

'Well, in that case, hello there, Gary. You've shaved off your beard.'

'Thought I'd go for a softer look.'

'Makes you look like a woman. By the way, you still owe me four hundred quid.'

'God! Do I? Does he?'

'Yep. Took my cash, and then my cat.'

'No! Bastard!'

'You said it, girl. I loved that cat, too. I'm looking for a nice one like yours, now. Man, not cat.'

'Cat might be simpler.'

'Oh yes?' says Sinéad. 'So says the woman with two. Men, not cats. Is your actual husband available by any chance? You've obviously got good taste in blokes.'

'Oh.' I falter.

Her face falls.

'Oh no!' she exclaims. 'Oh Jesus! Really bad joke. Like, really, really bad joke! I'm sorry pet, I'm an eejit. I'm supposed to be looking after you, not upsetting you.'

'Don't worry. It's just that my husband's a good man. I don't not love him. I've never not loved him. I still love him. I just love Angus as well. He's a good man, too.'

'Two good men,' she says. 'What's not to like. I'd give my right arm.'

'You wouldn't if you had any sense, I promise you. But you can have my left one if you like. It bloody hurts.'

Sinéad chuckles and says, 'You are seriously making

my day.' She slides a soft, black half tube along and under my raised arm, positions it carefully before securing Velcro straps across the top of it. She asks, 'How does this feel? It should be nice and snug but not too tight.'

'It's fine.'

'Good. We just need to attach this bit around your neck and then we're all set.' She clips the sling into place. 'There we go.'

'Thanks.'

She steps back and surveys me like the job well done that I am, for her.

'What will you do now?'

'We're supposed to have another two days here but I just want to go home. I want my kids.'

'Go home then, wee love,' says Sinéad, quietly. 'And see if you can't sort it out from there.'

'But they're away with my husband, staying with friends. They're not back until next Friday.'

Sinéad says, 'Next Friday, then. Be home.' On my good arm, she places her hand, which is warm and soft. I would dearly curl up in its palm and shut my eyes and stay there; for months, if need be. She says, 'You take good care of yourself, Lucy. You're a card and your man here's a dreamboat. It's going to hurt a hell of a lot more than your arm.'

* * *

When it came to it, I thought about lies and I thought about half-truths. I thought about them all the way during the journey back to London. I thought about options and compromises. I went around and around in circles but it was no use: I could not imagine settling back into a good life without Angus and I could not imagine Angus being part of a good, settled life. I thought about Einstein, who said that you cannot solve a problem with the same thinking that created the problem in the first place; and I thought about the problem itself as I lay awake for the last time, on my back and in pain, in *Verity*'s warm hold.

I considered for the briefest of moments pouring cold water, scorn – anything – over all that Angus and I had in an attempt to quench the fire and belittle our love. I could not do it. I couldn't tell Angus that I did not love him enough; that he was too old and I too young and we were thus unsuited. I could not argue that he was too set in his ways and I in mine; that my life was one shaped by the demands of youth while his was inclined toward autumn. I could not, would not, lie.

I could, however, tell him that he was the most beautiful man I had ever laid eyes on, and I did. He held his fingers to his lips, to silence me, but I continued. I told him that I am spoken for (whether or not my husband chooses to speak up); that my children need me more than he does, and that these are ties that bind me to a life defined by earlier promises. I told him that my love for him had not run its course and likely never would. It simply had nowhere to grow and could only deform in a space too small for it.

Except I'm not sure I said it as clearly as that.

I said, 'I love you, and I will always love you, as I have never loved anyone else.'

When I reached for him, he declined. He turned his head backwards and sideways, as a baby does when refusing from a proffered spoon the food it does not want.

He said, 'Oh my God, is this it?'

'I think it is.'

He faced me squarely, staring, as if I had just struck him.

'Oh God.'

Then he pulled me to his chest, hard, and wretchedly, so that my bad arm wrenched and I flinched, banging my leg into the coffee table sharply enough that for some time afterwards a coin-sized bruise prospered colourfully on my shin. I ignored the pain, as I had ignored it on occasion in bed when a limb became stuck or a joint strained, when my hair caught accidentally beneath Angus's palm, or a pinch of skin was trapped under his thumb as he moved against me, greedy, heavy, happy.

He said, 'Oh, nutcase,' and he began suddenly and violently to shudder. It was as if, right there and then, his body went to war, vibrating from within as though preparing itself for battle with information it could not bear.

And then, he howled. He howled in such pain and fury that for days afterwards, I couldn't get the sound of his sorrow out of my head. It replayed itself, a persistent intercession and unwelcome – just one of many forms of torture that were to follow. And as he did so, with a jolt I remembered hearing a lion declare himself in the night, when I was travelling in Africa with Mark years earlier; and just as the basso profundo snarl that woke us in our tent induced immediate, catatonic, terror, so Angus's distress did the same. It filled and then obscured the space between us, saturating the room, the boat, even the view of the river; dumbing down the outlines of the buildings on the other side of the water.

Afterwards, he sank back into the sofa, spent and disbursed, and taking my hands in his, he said – with no less desperation but quietly now, as if reminding me all over again of his range and contrasts – 'Tell me at least that I will see you.' I shook my head and he said, 'I know you're right. I understand. I do. We always knew this could happen. I promise I won't make it harder than it is.' He was shaking just as he had with the fever that time – when he juddered in my arms like a pneumatic drill and pleaded, childlike, 'Why am I so cold?' – and I realized he was in shock.

I collected a rug from the basket and with difficulty I

wrapped it around him, and he wrapped his arms around me. We wept a good while.

He said, 'But what about your things?'

I said, 'I can probably get them into a couple of large bags.'

He said, 'But your arm.'

I said, 'I'll manage.'

'I'll drive you home.'

'No.'

He said, 'I wanted it to be for ever.'

There was only one thing left to do after that. Away from *Verity*, along the gangplanks and on to the Embankment I walked. I hailed a cab and in its overheated interior keeled sideways like a widow newly apprised of her state.

The early afternoons are the worst. I walk around my house, putting things away. Just as my relationships with the people who live in it have changed, so my rapport with the house itself is less easy. We do not connect as we once did. In the shower, I am surprised when the spray hits me at an angle I do not expect. Angus's fridge door opens right to left, ours, left to right, yet I find myself trying to open ours the wrong way, tugging at the hinge side only to remember that I am at home, my proper home, the one I helped to create. I reach into the cereal cupboard for a box of muesli that differs from the one I eat with Angus. 'What are you doing here?' I want to ask. 'I'd forgotten about you. You are not the one I want.'

Sometimes I wake seeking a familiar pool of light from a window to my left. But it's not there because the window to my left is on *Verity*. I would expect to realize immediately, then, where I am. But the confusion is immense. It no longer occurs to me straight away that I am waking at home, in the bed I have slept in for so many years: these days, I am so stupefied with grief it takes time for the penny to drop, and when it does, there is no relief. My brain is rewiring itself. Now, my mind is a jumble of opposing cutlery drawers and hot taps and light switches. I need to remind myself when I go out, of the code for our burglar alarm. I anticipate shadows where there are none. I am no longer certain how much light to expect, or from which direction it will come.

There are times when I miss Angus so badly I think I will be sick. Constantly, I feel weak. My body is flimsy, my movements uncertain. Food is painful to swallow. Cooking meals, answering texts, going outside – it all seems impossible to contemplate. I walk to school and back twice daily but in the playground I meet no eyes, say no hellos: I take to wearing sunglasses, even in grey weather. The aim is for no one to speak to me and on the whole, they don't. If I sense amity, I avoid it.

At home, I revert to easy dishes. Beds remain unmade. A revelation: most things, it seems, can wait. My aims are rudimentary. If the children are fed and clean, and warm enough at night, then that is enough. *Ça suffit.* I am doing well. We will all survive another day. But I am not doing well at all. There is something primitive about all of this that is not remotely assuaging. This is not some cheerless bad-weather assignment, it is meltdown.

New low points are surpassed all the time. Whilst my children eat boil-in-the-bag fish and frozen peas for supper (these precious children for whom, when they were toddlers, I mashed organic salmon with unsalted butter and pesticide-free broccoli), I am remembering Angus whisking eggs for a perfect cheese soufflé, which he served with asparagus and we ate on the sofa, watching *Antiques Roadshow.* And it strikes me that if people think it is sex that matters most in extramarital affairs, and someone else's bed is where the rights and wrongs are located, they should consider how easily ruined you can be by the gift of a lovingly made supper – or the failure to prepare one. So just at the moment when it seems no self-reproach could be more potent than the remembrance of Angus's mouth on my belly in the middle of a school morning, his cheese soufflé comes to mind whilst I feed my children rectangles of plastic-encased cod, and I feel – rightly – condemned.

'Mummy,' Miranda enquires, 'why aren't you eating, too?'

Occasionally, very simple things can nourish.

I sew some buttons on to a cardigan for Miranda, a garment that has been a long time in the mending pile, and if I don't mend it now, she will grow out of it, giving me something else with which I may berate myself. I repair a torn sleeve on a school sweatshirt of Mel's. I patch a pair of Mark's jeans as well, with a square of denim cut from an old pair of mine. I survey my work afterwards, feel some small sense of accomplishment. The feeling is short-lived. That it should come to this – a couple of shell buttons and a penitential patch. I would patch over my heart if I could. Sew it into itself, with double stitches.

I lie on the sofa. Angus's was softer than ours is. Bigger, too. I think about the work I am not doing, the clients who want photographs of their children and dogs, and who are starting to lose faith in me – just a little, perhaps, but enough that it is slightly perilous to my reputation, which until now has been comfortably reliable. I wait for time to pass or to overtake me, I neither know nor care which. The house is silent without Mark in it and with the children at school. My ears are buzzing gently. The windows we installed at such expense when we first moved in are effective. There is no sound from inside the house and none from without, not a whoosh from the wind and nothing from the birds. Mark's world.

I can't listen to music.

There are a million things to do. A lot of people say

233

that: 'I've got a million things to do.' But maybe I do now, so long have they been undone. I don't know where to begin. There are emails marked '*Unread*' in my inbox, calls to return. There is laundry and piles of clobber around the place. There are mud-caked boots in the porch and yet another bin-bag of outgrown clothes destined for Oxfam, an affront every time we come and go. It might take fifteen minutes to clean the boots, one car journey to remove the bag. I never do either. We are out of green vegetables. There are carrots, but carrots are not a proper substitute. Really, I need to buy Melanie some new school shoes. She's harder on footwear than her sister is; she drives holes into her soles and grinds down the backs of heels. That means a trip into town.

Yet still I lie here, pathetic, noticing vaguely the crackle of the sofa cushion beneath my head as I glance from a recumbent position out of the window at the garden. It is, I observe, the garden of a depressed custodian. Like unkempt hair, the honeysuckle has become sharp and straggling, its flowers long gone. I should have cut it back months ago. The thick stalks of summer geraniums in large terracotta pots became woody and desiccated long since. Now, left out too long in damp weather, they are sodden. The trees are grey and shiny with the perspiration of rimy weather and the grass everywhere too long. It will remain too wet now, either with rain, or frost, to cut until the spring. It occurs to me that flowers and colour would make little difference to my life. There is no improvement to my mood when the sun shines. When it does, I feel vaguely offended.

On the wall of the barn, across the yard, I can see Mark's bright orange safety jacket, the one he wears when chainsawing with me. It is hanging on a large wooden peg that he carved for himself some years earlier on a beautiful midsummer evening. I had given him a sharp, curved knife for his birthday. He had been very pleased at the time but it had lain unused on his workbench for a while, until that evening.

I was in the garden. I remember he called to me from the open front door, 'I've made some tea. And what if I bring out that nice cheese we bought? Do you fancy some?'

In the honeyed early-evening sunshine, Mark sat on a tree stump and carved. The wood was ash, easy to work through. I donned my heaviest gardening gloves and pulled a few obstinate weeds. I noted the flowers and silently gave thanks for my life: foxgloves, meadowsweet, violets, wild orchids. Miranda, Melanie, Mark.

By the time the light was almost gone and the birds had retreated to their high perches in the beech trees, Mark had fashioned a large peg.

'Nice, isn't it,' he said, passing it to me to examine. It was soft and smooth to roll around the palm of the hand. I said, 'It feels like velvet.'

He made a couple more things after that; a shoehorn, shaped from a conveniently curved piece of sycamore, and a rough-hewn bowl for the girls to put things in. Currently, it holds some jigsaw pieces that have become separated from their neighbours, and a few stray hair slides.

It was lovely, that evening.

We have had a lot of them over the years, Mark and I; lovely evenings.

Now, if I see or hear Mark coming over to the house from the barn, I get up from the sofa and busy myself with something. But if I don't make it in time and he finds me there still, he never exploits the opportunity I have given him, increasingly to consider me contemptible. He is only ever kind.

I have not seen Angus for two months. We have agreed not to text or email one another. Once only, he phones me, and leaves a message. He says, 'I just wanted to hear your voice.'

I hear his, constantly.

'I'm jealous of your kids.'

'Silly old thing.'

'They get you all cosy after supper. They get you at breakfast-time.'

'Breakfast is a scrum.'

'You make hot chocolate for the twins at night.'

'Only occasionally.'

'I'd like hot chocolate, too.'

'I make it for you when I'm here.'

'I wish you were here all the time.'

Now, he is here all the time.

I never brought him to my home, but he has managed successfully to be anywhere I look and every place I go.

It's my own fault. We saw each other too seldom for our liking and I made up for it in any way I could. In an ongoing virtual tour of my life, I took him everywhere possible, texts and emails bearing the details of my life at home, with others.

Fucking mobile phones.

Because of them we were rarely out of touch for more than half a day, wherever we were, whatever we were doing. Which means that wherever I am and whatever I am doing now, the memory of Angus is here – in every room, in every way. In the kitchen. In the bathroom (my back is against the towel rail, warm, but the recollections produce a chill: *'How's my darling today? xxx' 'Just out of the shower, missing mine. xxx'*). He is even in the bedroom, in the bed itself – Mark asleep beside me – where too often and ashamed (but not enough), I would respond to the ping of a text. At six in the morning, three in the afternoon, noon, midnight, lunchtime, bath-time, story-time, any time, any minute, any second that a twenty-four-hour day has ever produced, Angus has been available to me and I to him, only a keyboard away, with absolutely no regard for geography, business or circumstance. In the supermarket, in the car, alone and not alone; at lunch with my parents, or from bedrooms, various, in which Mark and I were billeted on occasional visits to friends. It never mattered where: the trick was to stay in touch. On the hill above Jay and Lisa's house, which lies in a dip without phone reception, in a screaming gale on New Year's Eve at 23.37, I emailed Angus my photo so as to catch him before we kissed the cheeks of other people, at separate parties where – freshly in love with one another, our relationship barely begun – we longed already only to be together. He entered my life and I absorbed him. He teased and provoked, gave and received, every single day and every single night for ten months since the evening we met. And now, the evidence of love is driven hard, hard, hard, in kilobytes, megabytes, words, photos, playlists and emojis – of winking suns and piano keys.

The emails I kept, some more precious even than the ring Angus gave me. As for the texts, I should have deleted those as we went along but I never did. I have, now. Something had to go. Something had to be jettisoned, so there is a place I can be where Angus is not.

* * *

In the shower, on school days, is where I scream. I turn the lever until the heat is more than I can stand. I wait until my skin burns scarlet and the top of my head stings. Afterwards, my forearms itch so much I scratch them until they bleed.

The skin around my eyes is pink and raw. Each time I cry it gets worse. I apply some E45 cream to the blotches but it makes no difference, not even after two or three days. In the medicine cupboard, I find some time-expired steroid cream. *'Do not apply to the delicate skin around the eyes.'* I smear it on. Overnight, the blemishes fade. I cry more, apply more; it is the wrong thing to do but my eyes look better for it. Betnovate and tears: who would have thought them such a harmonious match.

After showering, I put on Angus's old Guernsey sweater: he lent it to me once to keep me warm on a late journey home, told me later to keep it and enjoy thinking of him whenever I wore it. All I want is him. His sweater is the nearest I can get.

I could work but I don't. It is many weeks since I accepted a new commission. Life is very quiet. I take myself upstairs and lie on the bed that has nothing to do with Angus. I set the alarm so I will be ready to collect the twins on time, bury my face in his thick folds of wool, and cry. After that, I sleep.

* * *

After a storm, there is always clearing to be done. In the winter, when the gales come, our yard is strewn with dead sticks and stray branches. We collect them up, and in the small field behind the house we make a pile that will be a bonfire when the right day presents itself. When it does, in the spring sometime, the girls will help to keep it going, with enthusiasm and smaller sticks. They will perform a haphazard dance around the fire's perimeter, poke unnecessarily at its edges with long twigs, and jump to its louder cracks, as the wood splits and twists in the flames, alive one last time after a season of lying dormant. Heat will belt out in a jubilant release of energy following a winter of postponement.

Mark takes the pitchfork, inserts its tines into a mess of elder, and tosses the straggling, anorexic branches on to the fire. He says, 'October already. We're so late with the fire this year.'

'I don't understand why we didn't burn all this in the spring.'

'We had other things to contend with.'

I stare into the flames for a while. The juices from the elder hiss as they evaporate.

I say, 'Why didn't you stop me?'

'You were gone,' he replies, 'within ten minutes of meeting him.'

'You could have stopped me.'

'Nothing could have stopped you. It was like watching the weather close in.'

I remember it. Immediate and heedless, devoid of rationale. How blatant it was, our beginning; how lacking courtesy, compared with mine and Mark's.

'You didn't even try, though.'

'I never thought for a minute it would amount to anything.'

'But you just let me go.'

'You chose to go!'

'Because I thought you didn't care.'

'And I thought you didn't love me enough.'

'You had a choice, too, Mark.'

'Yes, and I made it. I thought if I allowed you the freedom to do what you needed to do—'

'Wanted to do.'

'Okay, wanted.'

'Well, there's a difference.'

'I thought if I allowed you that freedom, then at least I'd know that if you came back it was because you chose to and not because I'd forced your hand. I'm married to you but I don't own you. I mean, what did you want me to do? Torch his piano? Beat him up?'

'Of course not!'

'Which, by the way, I could easily do if the need arose; I could take him down, no problem.'

'Right.'

'And which I never would, because I'm not a Neanderthal.'

'No.'

Mark sighs.

'So, what else could I do? Beg? Fuck that! Throw you out? Not really. Would I have been much more the man in your eyes, if I'd done that?'

'No. Well, maybe. I don't know.'

'Okay, so tell me how any of those things would have helped.'

'I don't know.'

Mark says, and his voice neither rises nor falters, 'Listen to me, Luce. What if I'd objected? Think about it. I could have put you in a position where you might have come to hate me. And I might have lost you that way, and then the twins would have lost us being together, too. At least this way I was part of it and not just some loser in the background not knowing what the hell was going on. At least I had some control – what little was available to me.'

'I could not have done that, in your shoes.'

'I would have said exactly the same thing, before. But it's not that simple. We're a family. And you don't know until it happens to you, how you'll react. Some of it is knee-jerk. You didn't expect to behave the way you did, either. We all do things we would never have imagined. A lack of obstruction was the only response I could think of at the time, and I had to think on my feet. If I couldn't stop you, I was damned if I was going to try, and risk failure.'

'So, is that what you have been doing all this time? Not risking failure?'

'Partly. Mainly, I've been trying to hold us all together. Someone had to.'

Something I always wondered, and did not care to ask.

'Did you never hate him?'

'Once.'

'When?'

'When he took you to the concert that first time. I thought, "You slippery, mendacious bastard. Offer my wife something I can't, why don't you."'

'Oh, Mark.'

'It's okay. But it's the one thing I didn't feel I could say no to – your listening to music with someone. I didn't want you to feel as locked in by me as I do by my deaf-ness. I never wanted to co-opt you into my world. It's not the greatest place to be.'

'You never have.'

'Come on, Luce. I'm bloody difficult to live with at times, I do know that.'

'That's not because you are deaf.'

243

'No, it's because I am so determined not to be.'

With the fork, he pitches more elder on to the fire, then prods at its charred centre. I pick up some dry ash branches and toss them into the mix.

I say, 'I always thought that you were so much the better person.'

Mark frowns.

'It's true,' I continue. 'I felt that whatever I did I could never match you, that I would always be insubstantial. I've always felt that, beside you. I've done nothing important with my life except have the girls.'

'That's crazy. You're a good photographer.'

'Not really. You're the one with the career.'

'Thanks to you. And probably at the expense of yours.'

'Do you mean that?'

'Yes,' he says. 'I do. Do you think we would have this,' he gestures from the field towards the house and the yard, 'if it weren't for you? Do you think I would have been able to do what I do if it weren't for you? I'm not just talking about you being a mother at home, so I can get on and paint, though God knows that's enough. I'm talking about those times when something happens to make me feel really deaf and really isolated and a real fucking outlier, and the single person that makes the difference, that makes it bearable and even funny at times, is you.'

'And then I do this. I make you lonely.'

'Luce,' he says. 'I live in silence.' He pauses. 'Do you think I could feel any lonelier than I already do?'

'I am so sorry.'

'Don't be. There is nothing that anyone, not even you, could do to make the feeling much more potent than it already is. That's why I reacted as I did. I couldn't stand how confined you seemed; it was just too close to home.'

'Why didn't you say so?'

'You couldn't hear a thing at the time.'

I say, 'This will sound so hollow but it's the truth. I only ever wanted to love you.'

I did. I wanted to love Mark and I wanted the world to be kind to him. I felt that with me, it would be. I wanted to make something soft and amenable of myself and give it to someone else. I was terrible raw material but it's what I hoped.

And I wanted to marry. A bit of a separatist I might be, but solitary? No. Loneliness, I wanted it to stop. At the time I met Mark, no obvious road lay ahead. There's no doubt I fell for him hard and fast but when Di asked me once, around the time the twins were born, 'Why Mark, especially?' I answered before I could even think about it, 'Because he was there.'

Because he was there. It truly wasn't meant the way it sounded.

Yet how far might I backdate the original sin, that kernel of my shame? *Because he was there.* When I accepted his proposal in the kitchen, tea towel in hand? That chilly August night in Oxford under the cherry tree? I recollect what I said to Angus, over our first supper: 'Isn't it usually the case, that it is more about oneself than the other person?' After all, Angus and I loved one another with a greed and self-absorption I still find hard to square with otherwise reasonably generous, outward-looking human beings.

'I belong to you but you don't belong to me ...'

I shudder.

Mark says, 'You have loved me, mostly.' He holds out one arm. 'You're cold. Come here.'

He puts his arm around me. He has not done this for a long time. My mind with a mind of its own hurls backwards to our first moments – mine and Angus's. I can see him now as he approached me that first afternoon on *Verity*, one hand raised to stroke my face, fingers curling softly. I see that beautiful smile of his, the man I have loved unlike any other – see how he held my gaze as his hand rose and then fell. I remember how he traced me so often with his hands, and drew me so completely; how he captured me in every mood and light – and I, him.

My throat constricts, for I am sick with longing. I shut my eyes and inhale the smell of Mark's shirt, which is woody and cool, and think of Angus, always warm to the touch.

I look at my husband. His hair is greying and his eyes

are beginning to crinkle much more noticeably around the edges. He dislikes this but I don't because those lines tell the truth: that Mark is older, and weary, and handsome still. I understand things that before I did not. I realize that Mark is unafraid of truths I have been so keen to deny; that we are born alone and die alone, and that despite our mating and our passions we live alone too, whether alongside another person or not. Angus understands this as well: he learned earlier and more brutally than most people do, what it means to be entirely recast, alone. Perhaps his solitariness, and Mark's, is their most defining feature – the characteristic that makes them closer to one another in spirit than either of them could ever be to me.

Mark says, 'You look exhausted.'

'I can't sleep.'

I wake three, four, five times a night. Too often still I reach for Angus and though I understand immediately it is not him, sometimes it is still such a shock it makes me cry.

I would know Angus even in the gloom of a moonless night, from the curve of his broad back and the way he takes my arm and wraps it around his chest, tucking it under his own arm and folding my fingers into his hand. He strokes my fingers gently with his own, idly brushing my wedding ring. Occasionally, he even rubs the ring itself, and when he does this I wonder what he is thinking.

If we are lying the other way, me with my back to him, he kisses the nape of my neck, I curl my back closer into his belly and with his arm around my waist, he pulls me close. Our legs knit together and his foot will gently surf the downward slope of mine until his toes come to rest under my arches. We fall asleep that way, most times. In the morning, heat and the need to stretch having separated us in the night, he strokes my hip and thigh. Back and forth, back and forth, in long, slow arcs. He keeps it up for a good, long time, if I am lucky, whilst I lie completely still, feigning slumber, like a rabbit in a field pretending invisibility, electrified, waiting for a threat to pass – except that there is no threat; I am simply enjoying the sensation, electrified also.

Or, was.

Oh, Angus. Damn it all.

Tears come, silent and full. I think how the duvet always travelled his way; how he rolled himself into it so that I had to nestle close in order merely to stay covered; how even in sleep, I was in his wake. In bed, as in our entire relationship, he wanted my proximity always and he composed – or so it seems, now – an arrangement of sensual and aural connections so entire that it was impossible to experience anything less than profound intimacy. The piano, the sofa, the kitchen table, the bed, the bath: instruments, all of them, played to perfection, and with real heart.

When I wake beside Mark, I am disappointed. Yet there is something else too, a consciousness so sharp it feels physical, of white-hot relief and gratitude. *My husband has not left me. He had every reason to go and yet he chose to stay.* I watch him sleeping, oblivious, and even though I am toxic with misery each time I experience the split-second realization that he is not Angus, I place one arm across him. Remorse, not desire. I tell him that I am sorry and I still love him. Occasionally, I elaborate, for telling him only this feels incomplete. I tell him I still love Angus, as well. I tell him I missed the children like hell whenever I was on *Verity*, and I miss Angus like hell, now. I tell him how blank I felt towards him, how with Angus in my eyes I could see almost nothing and no one else. I explain how frightened I am – that this effect might never go away, that my sight will remain for ever obscured. I say things I will share with no one but Mark, and that Mark will never hear. I say that I do not know how to be, any more; that I am no longer the woman I was, no longer the wife.

I say, now, 'Can you forgive me?'

'There's nothing to forgive. I didn't consider the scale of the risk.'

'But I still did something selfish, something wrong.'

'You fell in love with someone else. I could have done much more to help us both. You can say it was my fault it happened in the first place, or yours, or both our faults, or nobody's. But you can only forgive someone if a wrong has been committed and I don't think you've committed a wrong, and I don't think I have, either. I don't think right or wrong is a helpful way of looking at these things. We're human. We both just got lost for a bit.'

Mark inhales, deeply. 'One day,' he says, 'when we're older and life is giving us something else to worry about, all this will just be a sentence in a conversation – about that miserable year we had, way back when. Chances are, in time, we may not even remember which year it was.'

'But the children.'

Mark says, 'Don't cry, Luce.'

'They're seven next month.'

'And they're fine. You'll give them a lovely birthday party, as you always do.'

'I went away.'

'Not so they really registered, or not terribly. And they had me. Anyway, you're here now.'

'I should have been here all the time'

'That's unrealistic. Few mothers are.'

'Mine never was. Nor Dad. But they're lousy examples.'

Mark says, 'You know, one thing occurred to me a while back.'

'What was that?'

'All that cooking you said Angus did. Playing music to you, wanting you to be happy. All that attention he lavished on you, like you were the only thing that mattered. I honestly don't think it was a lover you needed. It was a parent.'

We tell the girls it's time they came out to the field for some fresh air, before it gets too dark. We bribe them with the promise of fire-toasted crumpets. They oblige, and for a while, four-square, we stand around eating and chatting. When the temperature starts to drop and our breath becomes visible in the air, they ask if they can return to the television.

I look across the field. I feel like a boat that sailed away. For a short while, the land was still in view but so quickly, it disappeared out of sight. Now, I can see it again but it is indistinct and uncertain. I cannot know whether I would feel differently had I turned around and begun to sail back to shore sooner than I did.

What hubris, that I could have imagined myself immune to the effects of another person, capable of sustained control over a lawless body and ungovernable mind. What conceit made me believe I was better equipped to cope with emotions so powerful they hurl other people to the side of their lives? What convinced me that I could possibly choose how much or how little I might come to care? I know I thought myself more able to avoid the fallout than anyone else, I know I believed I was tough. I thought this might be one of those adventures that life presents very occasionally and that I could deny the feelings, bury the feelings or manage the feelings; that I could help myself to them when I chose. I did not know that, in ways I could never have imagined, I would be consumed; that it was not the time I spent with Angus that counted as much as the space he now inhabits in my heart and my life. What I did know all along, and yet denied, was that an ending of some kind was written into the DNA of our situation, and the scales were never tipped in Angus's balance. Our love might have been the biggest thing that ever happened to us but it was mostly confined to a few cubic metres on a river, where all change and movement went on outside. We both knew that. We knew it could hurt us. I had no idea how much. I'm such a fool.

Evening is upon us. I'm tired. It's so episodic, this business of remembering. It comes in waves, how I got from there to here, but the things I do remember – every so often they hit me with such violence that I am floored, a casualty of my own recollections. Unexpected love is like a blow to the head with a blunt instrument. It can come from any direction and with a degree of force well beyond the ordinary: if only, like a cyclone, it were forecast, we might be prepared – but it never is, and we rarely are. That people so willingly condemn one another for being susceptible to it perplexes me.

Angus was the perfect pool, far-reaching and still,

inviting me to dive in and break the surface, beneath which I would find relief from the heat he produced in me. Just as cool waters bid the fevered, his invitation held the same sublime promise.

My memories of him in those early weeks are all defined by size: by the imposition of his height; his long limbs, strong and nonchalant; his steady hands. But also, they're defined by the magnitude of my longing for him. I thought he might have become scaled down, in time, by being mine. He never did. Familiarity never reduced him. I wish it had.

What I remember and what I don't: some of it is pin-sharp and some so opaque that I think I may lose my mind – not to the business of remembering but the effort of trying to make sense of it all. I know what has happened is real but my memories can still assume the qualities of dreams. Perhaps they are safer that way, at one remove. Images swim across my mind, like passion's drift: I kneel before Angus in the mirror, his hands in my hair. We watch each other in the glass.

Now, I know it is not events that leave their marks but our sense of them, those primitive recollections of how we applied ourselves to one another: the tang of skin or the spike of a fingernail as it brushed the spine. It is not where we went or what we did that remains but what it felt like and what that meant. I can taste Angus still. He catches in my throat.

People say things happen for a reason. I don't believe that. I think we're random organisms, just molecules bumping into each other in a universe whose further laws we may never come to understand. Here we are, sandwiched meaninglessly between birth and death. There is chaos and there is free will, and as far as I can see, that is about it. We justify our desires with rationale, which is understandable, but it isn't science and it isn't fate: it might at best be romance, that prodigious contaminant of better judgement. I could tell myself that Angus and I were meant to be but if that were true then just about everything else is meant to be, too, and I simply don't buy that. I think we are all accidents waiting to happen. It doesn't mean we have no choices. When you are involved in a collision with someone it is up to you what happens next. It is possible to smile and walk away. Numbers do not need to be exchanged. Anyone who claims otherwise is a liar.

As for any outcome, it is as insufficient as it is incontestable. What I have with Mark is overcast: I love Angus still, as he loves me. The light has faded, somewhat. I do not know if it will ever be all right.

We circle the field, not saying much. Before we climb the gate back into the yard, we stop and contemplate the view from outside the house, looking in. We do this occasionally – stand here in the chill, gazing at our glowing daughters, oblivious on the warm, blind side of glass. Lights are on in the windows top right and bottom left, and from them an amber luminescence emanates, beguiling in its suggestion of warmth. It is a sight that used to arouse intense yearning in me and the evocation of fairy tales in which the cold, hungry traveller chances upon a house in a clearing just when he or she needs it most. It promises sanctuary and hope, and therein lies its romantic power.

As Mark always says of our home, it's exactly the kind of place you would want to be if you weren't lucky enough to live here already.

He kicks at the fire. It is still burning but with less vigour now. He deems it safe enough to leave.

Acknowledgements

Love and thanks to my beloved family, Andrew, Clare, Jane and Celia St George, for the encouragement, humour and healthy derision that has kept me going during this absurdly long-haul project.